parABnormal Magazine

September 2024

Edited by H. David Blalock

parABnormal Magazine
September 2024

All rights reserved. No part of this book may be reproduced or transmitted in any form or by any means, electronic or mechanical, including photocopying or recording or by any information storage and retrieval systems, without expressed written consent of the authors and/or artists.

parABnormal Magazine is a work of fiction. Names, characters, places, and incidents are products of the authors' imaginations. Any resemblance to actual events or persons, living or dead, is entirely coincidental.

Story and illustration copyrights owned by the respective authors and artists.

> Cover illustration by Mat Kaminski
> Cover design by Laura Givens
> First Printing, September 2024
> Hiraeth Publishing
> http://www.hiraethsffh.com/

Visit http://www.hiraethsffh.com/ for online science fiction, fantasy, horror, scifaiku, and more. Support the small, independent press...

Vol. VI, No. 3, Issue 23   September 2024

parABnormal Magazine is published quarterly on the 15th day of March, June, September, and December in the United States of America by Hiraeth Publishing, P.O. Box 1248, Tularosa, NM, 88352. Copyright 2024 by Hiraeth Publishing. All rights revert to authors and artists upon publication except as noted in selected individual contracts. Nothing may be reproduced in whole or in part without written permission from the authors and artists. Any similarity between places and persons mentioned in the fiction or semi-fiction and real places or persons living or dead is coincidental. Writers and artists guidelines are available online at www.hiraethsffh.com. Guidelines are also available upon request from Hiraeth Publishing, P.O. Box 1248, Tularosa, NM, 88352, if request is accompanied by a self-addressed ***10 envelope with a first-class US stamp. Editor: H David Blalock.

Contents

Stories

6	Suzy Snowflake by Lance Loot
20	The Other Jennie by a.l. Dawson
37	Aveline's Apartment by Shikhar Dixit
53	Taking Jenny Home by Sarah Cannavo
68	For Serenity by Corrine Pridmore
77	DRUDE by Herika R. Raymer

Poems

19	Oblivion by Debby Feo
34	Ghosted by Jan Cronos
	A Portrait of Death in Grief & Brief by A. A. Alhaji
36	Trans-Allegheny Lunatic Asylum by Lee Clark Zumpe
52	What Happened by Denise Noe
	The Walled Garden by Jean-Marie Romana
98	Spectral Presence by DJ Tyrer

Articles

99	Brain Science Paranormal by R.D. Hayes
106	The Zen of Halloween: A Holiday of the Normal and the Paranormal by Gary Davis
112	She-Devil (1957): Hair Color and Sensuality, Sensuality and Horror by Denise Noe
129	On the History of Psychic Science by Sonali Roy

Illustrations

35	Ectoplasm by Hira Rashid

A Little Help, Please

In the world of the small indie press we fight a never-ending battle for attention to our work, as writers and in publishing. Here's an example: big publishers [you know who they are] have gobs of $$$ that they can devote to advertising and marketing. Here at Hiraeth Publishing, our advertising budget consists of the deposits for whatever soda bottles and aluminum cans we can find alongside the highways. Anti-littering laws make our task even more difficult . . . J

That's where YOU come in. YOU are our best promoter. YOU are the one who can tell others about us. Just send 'em to our website, tell them about our store. That's all. Just that.

Of course, we don't mind if you talk us up. We're pretty good, you know. We have some award-winning and award-nominated writers and artists, plus other voices well-deserving to be heard [not everyone wins awards, right?] but our publications are read-worthy nevertheless.

That number once again is:

www.hiraethsffh.com

Friend us on Facebook at Hiraeth Publishing

Follow us on Twitter at @HiraethPublish1

What???

No subscription to parABnormal Magazine??

We can fix that . . .

Just go here and order:

https://www.hiraethsffh.com/product-page/parabnormal-magazine-subscription

...also makes a great gift any time of the year

Suzy Snowflake
Lance Loot

"Anna, wait up!"

Emily trudged through the snow as swiftly as her short eleven-year-old legs would permit, her breath pluming out like a wispy phantom from the exertion. She spotted Anna several yards ahead, motionless and with her back facing her. Emily's boots crunched as she hurried to reach her older sister.

The forest was a pearly, glimmering winter wonderland. Endless rows of towering trees stretched skyward for the overcast heavens, their bare limbs long since robbed of their foliage and replaced with glistening snow shelves. The crystalline wilderness was serene as a lake at dawn, save for Emily's scampering.

"Anna! What're you looking..." Emily trailed off when she saw them.

Two monolithic, skeletal bur oak trees stood perfectly in line with one another, a truck's length of open space between them. Just beyond, the frosty terrain sloped downward to a place unseen. But the trees themselves weren't what caused Emily's blood to run as cold as the frigid forest air.

It was their faces.

Melded into the bark of each oak were a pair of ghastly visages. Dark craters formed the eyes while elongated, shapeless crevices resembled agape mouths wailing in silent horror.

Their bottomless stares bore into Emily, as if reckoning her like emissaries of the afterlife. She cried out and fell backwards to the fluffy powder as though she were about to make a snow angel.

Slowly, Anna rotated to face her fallen sister. A manic grin overwhelmed her features.

"Isn't this *incredible?*"

Emily folded to a sitting position, her face scrunched up. "Wh-what?"

"Oh come on, don't be an idiot, Emmy... don't you know what this is?" Anna asked. She regarded the land below, her hazel eyes glinting with excitement. "It's the forbidden place... *her* place... Suzy's Hollow!"

"Wait... 'Suzy' as in Suzy Snowflake?" Emily asked.

"Yup! The one and only... the myth, the legend herself!"

An icicle of dread pierced Emily at this revelation, however, curiosity got the better of her as she gazed past the twin sentinel oaks.

The expansive valley of Suzy's Hollow was a vast blanket of pure white, devoid of trees save for the rows outlining the perimeter. The hollow appeared to snake along like a sprawling snowy roadway. She spotted a faraway and in the distance, Emily saw a massive frozen pond, presumably foretelling the valley's end.

Anna shot a sidelong glance at Emily, a mischievous smile plastered on her face. "So what d'ya say, Emmy? Let's go check it out!"

"No way!" Emily exclaimed, leaping to her feet.

"What's the matter? Scared of little ol' Suzy Snowflake? Don'cha wanna help her build a snowman?"

"No, Anna, stop! Let's go home, okay?"

Anna shrugged. "Fine. You wanna go home, go ahead. But as for me..." She pirouetted around and skipped toward the looming bur oaks.

"*Here coooooomes... Suzyyyyy...*" Anna sang.

Emily propelled forward and seized a wad of her sister's coat. "Okay, I'll go... but only for a little bit, then we leave! And promise you won't sing that song anymore." She shuddered.

"Deal!" Anna said, already scurrying to the valley.

Emily followed, but as she crossed into Suzy's Hollow, she focused her eyes on the ground so as not to see the terrible tree faces.

"Wow... it's so beautiful!" Anna exclaimed.

Emily summoned the courage to look up and gasped. Suzy's Hollow was indeed breathtakingly beautiful. The field of snow was perfect, completely unmarred by animal tracks, and it glittered like diamonds in the glow of the waning sun. The distant lake was a kaleidoscope of gold and violet hues, more closely resembling a sheet of glass than a body of water.

They trekked onward in silence, taking in the alluring view with open-mouthed wonder. But as they reached the heart of the hollow, they spotted something that seemed a bit out of place: a lone tree, its bark entirely blackened as if smote by lightning, stood in stark contrast to the backdrop of scintillating white surrounding it. Its crooked limbs branched out in all directions like inky serpents writhing in agony.

The sisters cautiously inched toward the bizarre tree.

"Strange..." Anna muttered. "I didn't think I saw any trees in here."

Emily halted several paces short of the tree, fear gripping her heart like a yeti's paw. "Anna, we've gone far enough. Can we go back now, please?"

Anna was at the base of the tree, scraping at the charred bark with her fingernail. "Yeah, one sec, Emmy, lemme just..." She trailed off as a red stream dribbled where the bark flaked away, as if the tree were bleeding from a wound. Alarmed, Anna inspected the russet liquid smeared on her finger.

At the same moment, Emily caught a flash of movement in the tree and glanced up to see a tangle of raven hair drifting amongst the branches. It looked like a person, and it wore something white and airy, like billowy silk. It was near impossible to follow—it blended flawlessly with the black of the branches and the white of the snow accumulations as though it were just as natural to the landscape. But as it neared the tree's peak, the hair parted briefly, revealing an awful, blue-tinged face.

Emily screamed.

Anna spun and dashed to her sister's aid. "Emmy! What is it? What happened?!"

"Up *there*..." Emily whimpered, shakily pointing to the tree's top.

Anna scrutinised the tree but nothing was there, no sign of motion. "I don't see anything."

"But something was there, I swear! And its face... it —" Emily paused, a frisson of fear freezing her insides. "It was all blue, like it'd been out in the cold way too long."

She looked at her sister with pupils dilated to onyx marbles. "Anna... what if it's Suz—"

"Emmy, don't even say it! It's just a stupid myth to scare little kids, okay? That's it. She's *not* real." But as Anna gazed upon the blood-like substance dripping from her fingertip, she wasn't entirely sure if her words were meant to reassure Emily or herself.

She wasn't able to ruminate on the matter for long.

An icy wind, seemingly conjured out of nowhere, howled through Suzy's Hollow with a biting vengeance, penetrating the sisters' bones like a polar chill. They ran for each other, hugging to stave off the cold.

"What's happening?!" Emily cried.

"I don't know!" Anna shouted over the blustering squall.

Then a voice came, singing in a whispered, ethereal timbre.

"*Heeeeere cooooooomes...*" the voice crooned, mellifluous as a sustained piano note. The voice seemed to emanate from everywhere as though it was one with the bitter wind.

A stirring in Anna's peripheral vision caught her eye, and she followed it, glancing behind her—the powerful gale had swept up snow, creating vortexes of sparkling snow devils. They corkscrewed for several seconds before fading to white dust.

Emily started to cry, her tears freezing to tiny icicles on her raw cheeks. A subzero breath capered the nape of her neck, raising the tiny hairs there. It was like someone had heaved a great sigh down her back. She instinctively twirled around.

Glaring at Emily was the same horrible face she had seen, dangling from one of the tree's lower branches, placing their noses a mere foot apart. Oil-black hair framed the face in knotted curtains. The skin was a cadaverous blue as if it had dwelled in a freezer its whole life. The eyes were a pupiless milky grey like mouldering tombstones and its maw was curled into a ghastly grin, the teeth looking like cracked ice cubes jutting from purple lips.

Emily's face mutated to a mask of terror like the ones on the bur oak trees. Terror rooted her to the spot, her mind a panicked whirlwind.

The face opened its mouth. "...*Suuuuuzyyyyy...*" the voice continued, its melody married to the wind and reverberating throughout the hollow. The apparition's frozen lips danced in perfect synchronicity to the singing—it was the source of the voice.

A cloud of frosty air billowed from the thing's mouth and hit Emily like a rancid snowball, shattering her fugue state. Adrenaline surged and she spun, sprinting away like a reindeer pursued by a ravenous polar bear.

"Emmy!" Anna called out from behind.

Emily didn't hear. She didn't stop running until she flew past the bur oak trees and exited Suzy's Hollow. She doubled over panting, hands splayed on her knees. The image of the wicked, hypothermic face bombarded her brain, and she vomited into the snow as though her body were attempting to purge itself of the hellish experience.

"Oh my god, *Emmy!*" Anna cried, bounding for her sick sister.

"*Anna!*" Emily spluttered, tears cascading to her chin.

The siblings met in a tight embrace, warming their numbed nerves. They held each other for a minute, then separated and began the journey home. They plodded in silence for what felt like hours.

Emily was the first to speak. "It was *her*, Anna. I know it was."

"No, Emmy," Anna said, shaking her head.

"Yes. That... *face...*" She stopped, shivering as a snapshot of the milky grey eyes and purple lips came flooding back. "It was Suzy, Anna. Suzy Snowflake."

Anna stared at the ground, but didn't reply.

"And I think you know—"

"Stop!" Anna snapped. "Just *stop*, Emmy! I didn't see any stupid face, and to be honest, I don't think you did either! Okay? And for the last time... *Suzy Snowflake is not real!* There was no one else in the hollow. You just got freaked out by that crazy wind."

Emily looked at her sister like she'd slapped her, and her wide eyes brimmed with tears. Crestfallen, she dropped her gaze, landing upon the scarlet smear on Anna's finger.

"Hey, what happened? You cut your finger?"

Anna stared at the dark stain. It had started to dry, but was still noticeably tacky. A knot formed in her throat. "No, I didn't. It's... just tree sap."

But she knew it wasn't. Neither sister spoke another word the rest of the way.

***

That night, Emily was awoken by a peculiar noise.

Tap, tap, tap.

Groggy, she glanced about her room, but almost everything was shrouded in blackness. Pale moonlight spilled from the lone window on the opposite wall, affording meagre illumination to a small swath in front of it. The windowpane was completely frosted over by a sheet of ice.

Tap, tap, tap.

The sounds were coming from outside the window.

Emily's stomach dropped like a descent into darkness. The opaque rime on the glass made it impossible to discern who or what was on the other side.

Then, something began carving into the ice, making abrasive sounds like a dental pick scraping a tooth. Emily could only watch in helpless horror as the unseen claw slowly scratched a message onto the window. It read:

Come out and play with me.

Emily cried out and buried herself under the covers, anything to obscure her from the window.

Tap, tap, tap.

She whimpered, wishing with all her might it would stop.

Tap, tap, tap.

She covered her ears and squeezed her eyes shut. Eventually, the soporific demands of sleep eclipsed her mind and she drifted off.

At the same time, the taps at the window ceased.

***

The following day, Emily relayed the night's eerie events to her sister.

"It was just a nightmare, Emmy!" Anna exclaimed. "None of it actually happened!"

"It wasn't a nightmare, it was *real!*" Emily replied, her hands balling into little fists. "Same with everything yesterday, too! I told you we shouldn't have gone into that place, but you wouldn't listen to me! And now..." She stopped, goosebumps blossoming along her skin. "Now she knows where we live."

"That's *it*," Anna said, shaking her head. She stormed to the hallway closet and yanked out a pair of ice skates by their tied laces, followed by her winter attire.

"What are you doing?" Emily asked.

"What's it look like? I'm gonna prove to you that it's all just a dumb legend! That everything you think you saw was just part of your imagination!" Anna fixed Emily with a stern stare. "I'm gonna skate on that pond in Suzy's Hollow." She stuffed the skates into a backpack and slung it over her shoulders.

"No! Please don't, Anna! Stop!"

But she was already out the door, marching toward the winter wilderness. Emily hastily donned her cold-weather garb and trailed after her.

"You can't go in there! Please, listen—"

"Shut up, Emmy! I'm going and you're not gonna stop me!"

They wandered through the woods, retracing their steps in the snow from the day prior. Emily was terrified but knew she couldn't allow her sister to venture into Suzy's Hollow alone. She reluctantly followed, hoping to the stars that Anna would come to her senses and turn around.

But that hope shrivelled and died as the twin bur oak trees loomed into view, their faces silently screaming for them to forgo this doomed endeavour. Emily's veins ran cold with glacial rivers as the hollow, cavernous eyes drilled into her like an ice fisherman's auger. Anna faltered at the trees. Her breath rattled as she shook, and Emily surmised her sister's shaking to not be from the cold.

"Anna...?" she offered.

Anna refused to meet her sister's gaze, preferring to stare at her boots instead. "Well, you comin' with or what?" She trudged past the screaming trees without waiting for a reply.

Emily ran after her. "Anna, *stop!*"

Anna, apparently weary of dignifying Emily's pleas with responses, ignored her. Way in the distance, the tantalising gleam of the frozen lake swam into sight and she quickened her pace. Emily struggled to keep up with her older sister's longer strides, but she doubled her efforts when she spotted another landmark.

The blackened tree.

Anna halted before she got too close. Her eyes swept the contours of the tree's gnarled, pretzel-like branches with dread. She studied the faded wine-coloured smear on her finger, recalling how the tree had leaked onto her.

How it had bled onto her.

"Anna, please!" Emily cried, out of breath and stumbling to Anna's side. "Let's go back! We shouldn't be here!"

Anna spun on her. "Then go home for all I care, ya big baby!" she spat, then pressed onward, keeping a wide breadth between her and the tree. Her backpack bobbed to and fro as she went.

Emily started to follow, but froze when she saw movement. Something skittered among the upper echelons of the tree's snaking limbs like a frantic tarantula. It seemed to blend with everything like natural camouflage, making it impossible to determine what it was exactly.

But Emily knew. Her heart juddered against her chest as if it wished to burst from its cage and escape the ominous hollow. She tried to call for Anna but her breath caught in her throat, the only sound coming out like a frog's croak.

It started snowing.

Large crystalline flakes floated down from the grey heavens, kissing Emily's exposed face with their cold. As they made contact, the snowflakes melted against the warmth of her cheeks, dissolving into a sticky residue, tacking up the region around her eyes. She instinctively wiped her face.

Emily screamed when she saw her hand came away slathered with red.

Slathered with blood.

***

Anna, hearing her sister's shriek, twirled to assess the problem—the sight of Emily's gore-streaked face prompted an ear-splitting scream of her own. She wiped the melted liquid from her face, also coming away coated with blood. She held her hand out and watched in horror as snowflakes fell into her palm, their white shapes rapidly liquefying to scarlet pools.

This can't be happening, she thought, her mind whirling like a spinning Rolodex.

Anna glanced at Emily to see a ghastly figure with a mane of tangled black hair lording over her—her pallor went as white as the surrounding snow. "Emmy! Behind you! *Run!*"

Without another moment's hesitation, Emily bolted for Anna, her little legs pushing themselves to their limit. She crashed into her sister and they embraced, both of them blood-streaked and petrified.

"*Oh my god, Emmy!*" Anna cried, pulling her close as Emily began to sob.

The apparition stood rooted to the same spot, still as death. It was impervious to the persistent snowfall; the sanguinary snowflakes repelled away from the thing as though polar opposites. Its cloudy grey eyes gaped at the sisters unblinkingly.

Then its mouth creaked open, and the cracked lips danced along as though murmuring an arcane incantation. At the same time, the howling wind returned, blasting through Suzy's Hollow with cyclonic force. And with it came the voice, the voice of the wraith, crooning in the same haunting, faraway-sounding intonation as before.

"*Heeeeere cooooooomes…*"

Emily and Anna huddled against the powerful gale,

struggling to stay upright.

"What do we do?!" Emily shouted, her eyes streaming.

"I don't know!" Anna cried over the screeching wind.

"...*Suuuuuzyyyyy Snowflaaaaake,*" the voice sang. The apparition began to glide toward them, hovering over the snow's surface and leaving no tracks in its wake. Its wild raven hair spasmed in all directions from the wind.

Alarm bells blared within Anna. Escape from whence they came was no longer an option. Emily's face was buried in her shoulder, and she wrenched her sister free, towing them to the pond.

"We gotta move Emmy, c'mon!"

Emily obliged, allowing herself to be led along. She cracked open an eye and saw the wintry phantom slowly floating nearer. She screamed like a seal eviscerated by a killer whale.

"*Anna, it's her! She's coming!*"

"Don't look, Emmy! Keep going!"

They made it to the pond, clambering onto its frozen surface. Despite a layer of snow, the trek was still slick. A quarter of the way across, Emily slipped on a bare patch of ice and dropped, dragging Anna to the ground with her.

Anna banged her knee hard on the ice, moaning in pain. She quickly glanced up to gauge their pursuer.

But the apparition was gone—vanished into the bleak winter air. The wind was dying down as well, dwindling to a chilly zephyr. And then it disappeared altogether. The bleeding snowflakes gradually ceased their descent, too, fading away like smoke.

Anna's eyes swept about the hollow, searching for any sign of the thing, but found nothing. A sick feeling wormed about in her stomach. After enduring so much chaos, everything had gone too calm, too quiet. All was as still as a primordial beast encased in ice.

And she knew it was only fleeting.

This feels like the eye of a hurricane, Anna thought, her throat going dry.

"What's happening?" Emily whimpered; she rose to her knees unsteadily and studied the terrain. "Wh-where did she go?"

"I don't know," Anna replied.

"I wish we were home, Anna."

"We will be soon, Emmy. We just gotta—"

Anna shut her mouth when she saw it. A dark shadow, its umbral edges whorling like fog, was glissading toward them at the speed of an elk. It was shaped like a person, like a crime scene body outline.

But not just any person.

It's her, Anna thought, her breath hitching. *It's Suzy Snowflake.*

When the shadow met the pond, it seemed to drop out and disappear, like it was sucked under the ice to the freezing waters below. Anna stared where it vanished from, fearing the apparition would reemerge at any moment.

Emily, shuddering and looking at the snow, hadn't seen the shadow. *"Please...* can we go now?"

Anna opened her mouth to respond, but before any words could spill out, a chasm cracked open in the ice at her feet. A blue desiccated hand splashed from the fissure, clamping around Anna's ankle in an icy, vice-like grip. She shrieked a bloodcurdling cry as the hand dragged her under, down into the black water.

***

"*Anna!*" Emily screamed.

She scrambled to the opening and looked upon the ripples. The surface was like gleaming obsidian, and she couldn't discern anything beyond. She immediately plunged her hands into the freezing water, feeling around for anything that could be Anna. She felt a clump of something long and stringy. Hope flared in her gut like a firework.

Anna's hair—I found her! Emily thought.

She pulled with all her strength, expecting to be met with the resistance of her older sister's dead weight, but to her surprise, it came away as if weightless as seaweed.

It wasn't Anna's hair.

Emily gaped in horror at her handful of knotty, inky hair.

No. Please God, no.

Her eyes dropped to the hole in the ice. A face glared at her just below the water's surface, a corpse-like face with blue-tinged skin, milky grey eyes, and cracked purple lips curled into a rictus grin.

"*Cooooome out and play with meeeee...*" the voice sang, pealing from everywhere as though it were the mouthpiece of the hollow itself.

A blue claw shot out from the depths, its long arthritic fingers like talons as they sprang open. Emily screamed and fell back as the claw slashed violently, tearing through her winter garb and raking the flesh underneath. Emily's side burned with agony as if ravaged by vicious frostbite. There was no blood though, as if the wound had been instantly cauterised by the thing's frozen touch.

Emily wailed and crab-walked backwards. The face emerged from the black water and the apparition levitated several feet above the pond. It leered at Emily, the cataracts of its eyes glistening like wet flint stones. Its shimmering dress billowed like white-capped waves and its long hair licked the air like black flames. In a spidery hand it clutched one of Anna's ice skates.

"*If you want to take a sleigh riiiiide...*" the spectre crooned. Its maw broke into a wider sneer, its rows of ice-cube teeth cracking like popped joints.

Emily's brain blared sirens to flee immediately, and she obeyed, dashing away as though a woodland critter stalked by a bloodthirsty predator.

"*...Weeeee... the ride's on meeeeee!*" the voice finished. The apparition dove to the snowbank, and upon contact, melted into the person-shaped shadow. It slithered onward in rapid pursuit.

When Emily reached the blackened tree, an idea sparked. Rather than continuing straight on the same path, she hooked right and bolted for the treeline bordering the edge of the hollow. The wraith vaulted out of its shadow form, morphing back into the ghastly woman, shrieking and clawing at the air. Just as Emily put one foot beyond the hollow's threshold, the spectre struck with the ice skate, slicing her back open. She wailed in agony and somersaulted into the wilderness.

Emily raised her hands defensively, fearing to be sheared to ribbons at any moment, but nothing happened. She opened her eyes to see the apparition standing at the edge of Suzy's Hollow, just inside the line of trees. The trees were more like bars holding a prisoner captive within their cold cell.

But then, the wraith smiled and took a step forward. Emily, bloodied and teeming with pain, could only whimper and watch helplessly—her body was exhausted and could run no more.

Then it took another step.

Then another.

But as it crossed fully into the forest, a peculiar thing happened: the wraith began to fade like snow dust drifting off in the wind, its body dissolving bit by bit to sparkling snowflakes. Anna's ice skate dropped to the cottony snow, the blade wet and dark with Emily's blood. The last to go were the rheumy eyes, still blazing into Emily with an icy fervour, but then those disintegrated as well, and nothing remained of Suzy Snowflake.

It was over.

Volcanic sobs erupted from Emily as she lay on her back, her mind restlessly processing everything. It was all too much to bear and she sputtered as tears and snot streaked her face.

Scritch.

A scratching sound pulled Emily from her mortified stupor.

Scritch, scritch.

Panicked, she swivelled her head about, attempting to locate the noise's source whilst fearing the worst. It didn't take long to find.

To her left, a phrase was being carved into the bark of a tree, each letter appearing gradually as though scribed by an invisible claw. The message read:

Bringing all the joy,
Suzy's come to town.

Emily cast her gaze to the ground and shuddered violently. Weary and broken, she turned away from the inscription, grabbed her sister's ice skate, and crawled through the winter wilderness in the direction of her home.

Behind her, Emily could hear the howling wind kicking up once more in Suzy's Hollow, as though bidding her a frigid farewell.

Oblivion
Debby Feo

I'm stuck in limbo
Unable to move forward
No where and no one
Can be any help

What actions were done
To justify this
I had tried my best
To follow all rules

Where's my guiding light
Where is my earned peace
Forgotten, unknown
Slowly going mad

The Other Jennie
a.l. Dawson

The drive from Boston to Truro was easy for Aaron Halcrow. Sunny day, mild temperature, little traffic. Couldn't have asked for more in the middle of October. Except he could. Today was the day to put the finishing touches on the fentanyl article. The sooner he could meet his informant and tie up a few loose ends, the sooner he could have a little time to relax on the Outer Cape.

As he rounded the bend in Route 6, he saw the Mobile gas station on the right. Almost 11am. Right on time. Nightcap said he would be there, next to the dumpster at 11 sharp. Aaron smiled when he thought about where these drug dealers get their names.

He slowed down and pulled the old Toyota toward the side of the gas station where the dumpster was. No Nightcap in sight. Aaron turned off the engine and got out of the car. He had to pee, but he didn't want to miss this guy or get him spooked if he was not there right at 11. Nightcap was big on wanting him to be on time. Aaron leaned against the driver's door and breathed in the crisp fall air.

Ten minutes went by and no call. He pulled out his phone and punched in the number Nightcap had given him. After one ring, the voice said the number was out of service. Aaron wondered if Nightcap had gotten cold feet. He could finish the story without him, but the informant said he could give him the precise time and place where the yacht would arrive off the coast tonight. He was not in the mood to sit on a sand dune in the dark hoping to see a drug deal.

He mumbled, "Okay forget it, call him later, worst case... What's the worst case?" Aaron put a hold on the negative thinking until he got to the Airbnb and took a walk on the beach. He could smell the salt air and not a cloud in the sky.

Find the bathroom, then take it from there.

***

A half mile past the gas station, he saw the turn off for Airbnb on the right. The thought of sitting on the deck with a view to the ocean took the edge off of things. He was about make the turn when he noticed a sign to a rundown second-hand bookstore, *La Lumière de la Lune*, on the other side of the road. He'd driven past this spot many times in the past, but he'd never noticed it. *What the hell.* He turned left and drove the car into the bookstore's gravel parking lot. He'd buy a good mystery while waiting for Nightcap to call.

The faded yellow and wooden shingles were typical of the salt box architectural style of Cape houses. The place had a kind of quirky charm to it. More like a weather-beaten dune house than a bookstore. He got out and walked to an open doorway. Inside, the lighting was dim, and a musty smell hung in the air. He made his way through the cramped aisles until he came to a bookshelf labeled, *Legends and Stories of the Outer Cape*. One paperback title caught his eye, *The Other Jennie* by Céline Corbeau. A mist shrouded tower stuck by lightning decorated the cover. Aaron grabbed the paperback and walked to the check-out counter in the back of the store.

The woman at the register had dark, braided hair that fell over her shoulders. Her face had a hard to define ageless quality to it. He noticed how her slender fingers resembled those of a concert pianist. The chestnut skin color of her face highlighted the deep green of her eyes.

The woman spoke first. "You bought the last copy of the book."

"Yeah, looked interesting. The cover was kind of Cape Cod Gothic. Just what I needed, a good escape."

"I wrote it because it was a story that needed to be told."

"You're?"

She made the slightest of smiles. "Yes, I'm Céline Corbeau."

Aaron thought he detected a slight French accent. "You're French? The sign, your name?"

"No, I'm Creole. My grandparents were from New Orleans and moved up here and opened this store in the

1910s. Been in the family ever since."

Aaron was about to say he'd never seen it when his family spent their summer vacations on the Outer Cape. Instead, he said, "Nice to meet you. I'm Aaron Halcrow."

She offered her hand, and he took it. A deep warmth coursed through his body.

Céline gently pulled her hand away and said, "Halcrow, that's Norse, no?"

Aaron tried to snap out of what seemed like a paralysis. He managed to say, "It's Norwegian, but my grandparents were from the Shetland Islands."

"You see, we both have interesting backgrounds and stories to tell."

An odd remark. Before he could say anything a brown and white cat jumped up on the counter and nuzzled next to Céline. The cat's green eyes studied Aaron.

Céline whispered, "Jennie, it's not nice to stare at our guest."

Aaron gained a modicum of composure and said, "Ah, the same name as the book title. I thought it was Jenny, but you just said *sh nee*. So French." The second he said it he felt like a ridiculous school boy trying to impress a girl.

Céline just nodded, while the cat continued to study Aaron.

All he could think of saying was, "How much do I owe you?"

"Eight dollars."

He handed her his credit card, pretending not to be spellbound by this strange woman.

"Do you want the receipt?"

"No, I'm good. Thanks again. Looking forward to reading it." He put the book in his shoulder bag and walked toward the doorway.

As he stepped outside, he heard her call out, "Take care. When you finish the book, we should talk."

He turned around, but she was gone.

***

Aaron threw Corbeau's book onto the bed. He stepped out onto the porch of the Airbnb rental. It faced a salt marsh and behind the marsh was a copse of scrub pine and white cedar. Through the trees he could just make out ocean. Closing his eyes he could hear the waves crashing against the beach.

He knew exactly what he needed. Forget about Nightcap for now. Corbeau's book could wait. The ocean always lifted his spirits, and a walk along the beach was overdue.

The wind had picked up, but it was still sunny. Aaron left his back pack and shoulder bag on the bed and climbed down the porch stairs. He stepped onto a wooden walkway that led from the cottage toward the ocean. Marsh grass swayed in the breeze and nearly covered his whole body by the time he got to the tree line. The path then turned into a trail of beaten down moss. Tree roots stuck out from the earth, so he walked along the side of the trail to avoid them. The soles of his shoes felt warm. He thought there might have been a fire, but he saw no evidence of charred vegetation.

Seconds later Aaron saw patches of blue through the scrub pine. He picked up his pace despite a mist coming in from the ocean. The temperature also dropped the closer he got to the water. In his eagerness to get to the beach he'd left his coat in the cottage. He hunched his shoulders, rubbed his arms, and ploughed ahead.

The tree line ended on top of a dune. High tide, not much beach to walk on. The sun was hiding behind some fast-moving gray clouds. White capped waves inched up the dune. Still, the scene had its own fierce beauty. He thought about sitting on top of the dune for a while, but he was chilled to the bone. Reluctantly, he turned around to go back to the cottage. With luck, Nightcap would return his call.

Before he took a step though, a strange shape caught his attention. To his right, maybe 100 yards away, he saw what looked like a castle turret, the same as the image on the front cover of Corbeau's book. He had to check it out.

He turned around and saw only shadows of branches and fog everywhere. No trail.

With the tide so high, the only way to reach the tower was to cut through the forest. The mist had become a fog that swirled around him with each step he took. Twenty feet into the forest, Aaron wondered if he'd made a mistake.

He took a few deep breaths to stave off panic that was starting to creep into his thinking. He knew the tower was not far off. If only... Then he saw it. Not the tower, but a faint yellow light in the direction of where he thought the tower might be.

As he moved toward it, he realized the ground began to get warmer beneath his feet. Heat seemed to rise up from the ground and shoot through his legs. He moved quicker now, pushing aside branches, bumping into tree stumps, but he kept going.

The ground was no longer warm, it was hot, as if someone lit a fire beneath the earth. Suddenly, the trees ended, and he tripped into a small clearing, falling prone onto the ground. The earth became cool, almost cold against his body. He stood up and saw that he'd arrived at the base of a stone tower. Had to be at least 100 feet tall. It had vines and pine branches crawling up its base.

On the other side of the clearing, close to the tower, a yellow light flickered. He walked toward it. The clearing turned into a cracked asphalt parking lot where a pickup truck and bulldozer were parked to the side of a Quonset hut type of building. It looked like a maintenance shed from the 1940s or 50s. The light emanated from a small, smudged window next to a metal door at the front of the building. Aaron made his way across the lot, watching where he stepped. Jagged asphalt hunks were strewn across the parking lot. As he got closer to the building, he heard two growling voices arguing back and forth. Once he reached the door, he thought one of the voices sounded like... *Nightcap*?

He peered through the grime-covered window. A man sat at an old roll top desk in front of several metal filing cabinets. Standing over him with his back turned was a younger guy shaking his head. Aaron couldn't make out their words; they were more guttural noises coming out of their mouths. The voice of the guy standing up reminded him of Nightcap's phone voice.

Aaron pressed his body against the building, trying to make out their words, but he ended up slipping on a piece of asphalt. The voices stopped. He heard a chair move and the sound of one of them coming to the door. He managed to pick himself up just as the door opened.

A heavy-set guy in his 50s towered over Aaron. The man's blood shot eyes locked onto Aaron as if they were coils of rope. Aaron's heart raced.

The man broke the silence. "Why are you here?"

Aaron stuttered, "I saw that tower from the beach and wanted to check it out. Got lost in the woods until I saw the light and went toward it. Then I heard voices and hope to get directions from someone."

The man's eyes stayed locked onto Aaron. "That tower's a mistake. Put up years ago by a wealthy crack pot for some damn reason. It's in bad shape. You should stay away."

"Okay. Could one of you guys tell me how I get back to the road?"

"There's no guys. Only me."

As the man spoke, Aaron tried to size him up. He wore dirty work pants and a faded denim shirt. A name tag on the shirt pocket read, *R.I.P. Cerberus, Groundskeeper*. His voice was not Nightcap's.

"Oh, so you work for the National Seashore?"

"Something like that. I just keep a lid on things around here."

The man paused and smirked before he said, "The road behind the building will take you to the highway." He turned around and slammed the door. It sounded like a bank vault being locked up for the night. The light from the desk lamp went out. An inky blackness filled the room. The voices were gone.

Aaron knew the guy lied. If Nightcap was in there, the argument he thought he heard could have been about a drug shipment. Maybe about the trawler dropping off a supply of fentanyl tonight. Maybe the tower was a lookout point. A lot of maybes.

He spotted the road as he reached the rear corner of the building. A growl greeted him. Aaron froze at the sight of a large Rottweiler chained to a post. The dog bared its teeth but didn't bark. Instead, it let out a continuous deep growl as Aaron began to back up. Its feral red eyes stayed glued to Aaron. He couldn't look at the thing anymore without getting dizzy. He ran to the road without looking back.

***

When Aaron woke up, it felt like he was still in a dream. He looked at his phone. 9 am. He'd hadn't gotten to sleep until at least 4 am. What he had experienced yesterday and what he had read in Corbeau's book last evening had sent his mind into hyper drive.

He took another sip of coffee. According to Corbeau, the tower was transported from Boston to Truro in 1927 by some wealthy railroad exec named Aldridge. That part was true; he'd done his own web searches to confirm it. Everything else about the tower seemed intertwined with local legend and fragments of actual historical events. Why was it there? Some say it was to honor the Swedish opera singer, Jenny Lind, who came to Boston in the 1840s and supposedly sang from the tower to adoring crowds in the city. And supposedly Aldridge had the tower transported to the Cape, where his family owned much of the Truro seashore at the time. It was his homage to the 'Swedish Nightingale.'

Aaron got out of bed, coffee in hand, and stepped out onto the porch. The real bombshell in the book was not the tower's connection to Jenny Lind. It had to do with an ancestral relative of Céline Corbeau. Her grandparents had taken in their niece, 16-year-old Jennie Marchand from New Orleans, to live with them in their apartment above *La Lumière*. Unfortunately, tragedy struck when Jennie had witnessed opium smugglers on the beach close to where the tower now stands. Jennie told her grandparents about what she saw and eventually went to the police. Nothing was done about it, and a week later Jennie disappeared. She was never found. Corbeau made the case that, ever since then, her disappearance has been covered up. Local people invented the tale that on certain nights the ghost of Jenny Lind could be heard singing from the tower. People never talked about Jennie Marchand.

Aaron threw the last drops of coffee over the porch railing. Sounded like Corbeau made up her own tale. Still, something didn't fit, and it bothered him. Why would a crime from the 1920s be covered up today? Was there a connection between the drug smuggling in the 1920s and the fentanyl trade today? Or just a random coincidence? Also, what about hearing Nightcap's voice in that maintenance shed? Or was it his voice? Why no phone call from him?

Instincts told him Céline Corbeau could tell him more. He rushed back inside to get his car keys, oblivious to a pair of red eyes peering at him from the edge of the scrub pine forest.

***

As soon as he entered the bookstore, he heard a voice call out, "Aaron, back here."

How did she know it was me?

He walked to the back of the store where it opened up into a small atrium. Céline Corbeau sat a small table with a pot of coffee and freshly baked scones.

"I thought you could use some strong coffee and something comforting to eat after your ordeal."

Aaron cocked his head in wonderment but sat down to take her up on her offer. She poured the dark, thick brew into a ceramic mug. He didn't see any milk on the table but took a sip and then another.

"This is good. No, it's great. I don't drink it black, but it doesn't matter. I needed that."

Celine nodded and said, "I know you did."

"Okay, what's the deal? You knew it was me at the door, you knew I had a lousy night, you even knew I needed the coffee!"

Céline reached over and took Aaron's hand. "Let's not get into why I know. I think the time we have together would be better spent with me explaining what we need to do." Céline let go of his hand.

Aaron felt a warm current run through his body. He didn't know why, but he felt calmer. All he could think of to say was, "Yeah, explaining would be good."

Céline's tone changed. Her voice became that of a teacher to a student. "I assume you read through *The Other Jennie?*" Without waiting for an answer she began, "You could tell that the point of my book was not about this Jenny Lind Tower nonsense. The tower is real, as you know, but the rest of the stories around it are fanciful. The real story is about the crime done to my ancestor, Jennie Marchand."

"You're convinced her disappearance was a crime and not an accident, like a drowning? And it's actively being covered up today? Why?"

Céline was quiet. Aaron wondered if he was too direct with her, but he didn't have time to humor this nice but strange person.

She betrayed no surprise or anger at his questions. Calmly she said, "Your doubts make sense. If I had your life experience, I would have those same questions. But I have had a different experience and a different way of understanding this world."

There was another pause between them. Celine's green eyes met his and a kind of silent rapprochement passed between them. Aaron nodded for her to continue.

"Aaron, I'm going to say this once, and you can decide what you want to do." She said the words softly and without rancor.

He nodded again.

"In 1927 America, Jim Crow was in full bloom. I alluded to that in the book, but it bears emphasizing it to you now. No, they didn't lynch black men in Truro, but the police certainly did not think much of the testimony from a 16-year-old black girl, especially if she implicated white men in a crime."

Céline took a sip of her tea. Before she continued, the cat came out of nowhere and jumped up on Aaron's lap. Jennie curled into a ball with her eyes gazing at Aaron's face. He stroked her chin but focused more on Céline's narrative.

"Our family never made peace with Jennie's disappearance. There is no closure for me. She demands justice. She needs to be set free."

"What do you mean, set free? She'd be long dead by now."

"What is death? If no reckoning had taken place, Jennie's life, and others like her across this nation, will never be put to rest. That's why a being like Cerberus makes sure she cannot be free. Therefore, the truth about what happened to her will never be revealed."

Aaron blurted out, "You know that guy? I met him and he is one hell of a shady groundskeeper. I think he's part of a fentanyl smuggling ring on the Cape."

He was going to say more, but Céline cut him off. "He's a groundskeeper all right, but not the kind you think. I wouldn't be surprised if he and his enablers are trafficking in drugs, but I'm talking about a bigger crime here."

Aaron didn't know what to say. Probably the trauma of Jennie's death and the racism she'd dealt with in her own life made her go over the deep end.

As if Céline heard his doubts, she said, "If you don't believe me, I can show you what Cerberus is up to. We should go to the tower. The night sky will be clear with a full moon. It will be perfect for what we need to do."

Her offer was like a challenge to his own sense of reality. Yet, in a way it didn't matter if she was a bit off. She knew things and knew this area. Witnessing Cerberus orchestrate a major drug deal, which was the most likely scenario, would add something important to his article.

"Okay, let's do this."

Céline stood up and Jennie jumped up on the table. Both stared intently at Aaron, as if taking the measure of the man.

She said, "If we do this, no police. You follow my lead and listen to my instructions every step of the way. I will meet you at your lodging around 11:30 tonight. Do you agree?"

"Yeah, sure."

Céline turned around without saying a word and

walked over to a staircase. She was gone in seconds. Jennie stayed sitting on the table waiting for Aaron to be on his way.

***

The trek through the scrub pine forest was much easier this time. It wasn't just the moon light that helped them get to the tower. It was Céline. She knew this forest.

Once they reached the edge of the clearing, they stopped. They hadn't said a word to each other since leaving the Airbnb cottage.

Céline motioned to him to crouch down. Without taking her eyes off the tower Céline whispered, "Listen. Can you hear that?"

Aaron learned forward and closed his eyes. The air was still, but he heard a faint rustling of underbrush next to the base of the tower. Copying her lead he spoke softly, "I hear it."

"That's Cerberus getting ready. October 15th. It's the anniversary of Jennie's capture."

Aaron had kept his doubts at bay, but now he wondered if he'd made a mistake coming with her to this place. It was pretty obvious she was not quite right. Generational trauma can do that.

Céline continued, "Cerberus is inside the tower now. Follow me, don't say a word. When we reach the entrance, wait for what I have to say. I can't do this on my own."

At least he might see a drug deal going down, if in fact Cerberus was in the tower, and it wasn't some raccoon building a nest. Maybe Nightcap would be with him.

They crawled across the moss-laden clearing and reached the base of the tower in under a minute. Now Aaron could hear what he thought was Cerberus's voice muttering the same garbled phrase over and over again.

Okay, no raccoon.

The last 15 feet to the tower entrance was littered with twigs and branches. Céline moved like a snake on her stomach to minimize their noise. Aaron did the same. When they reached the entrance, Aaron saw an open doorway. Inside, on an earthen floor, Cerberus circled around a small fire pit. His arms swung back and forth, creating eerie shadows across the tower's stone walls. Whatever was going here wasn't a drug deal.

Céline whispered, "Jennie will try to rise up. When that happens. watch what I do first, before you act. You will know what is required of you, but you must wait for the signal."

He felt like he had a fever. Everything about this escapade was seriously crazy. Then he saw it. A hand popped out of the earth, and its fingers seemed to be grappling for something or calling for help.

Without thinking Aaron acted. He rushed into the shadow world of the tower, hoping to help whoever was buried. Cerberus roared and lunged for him. He heard Céline shout, "No, wait!"

Then everything when pitch black.

***

Aaron woke up on the couch of the Airbnb. His head throbbed like a hangover from hell. He looked around. Nobody. *How did he get back? Where's Céline? God, what had he done?* He staggered to the door and stumbled down the porch stairs to the car. No time for coat, no time check out. He had to get back to the bookstore and find Céline.

The car was unlocked, and a handwritten note was on the dashboard.

> Aaron do not waste time blaming yourself.
> This struggle is an old one and takes time.
> Our work will continue. Your story is part
> of a larger story. Believe that. I will see you
> back here next October 15th.
>
> Yours,
> C. Corbeau.

He couldn't take it in. Made no sense. He started the car to leave when he heard a meow. Jennie jumped from the back seat onto his lap.

"What are you doing here? Let's get you back to

Céline."

The cat curled up on his lap as he drove back to Route 6. He was about to cross over the highway to *La Lumière de la Lune* when he hit the brakes. Jennie let out an annoyed meow but stayed put on his lap. The bookstore was in ruins. Only the sign and part of the atrium remained standing. Police tape ran around the store grounds. Steam and ash hung in the air above burnt timbers.

Aaron stroked Jennie's head. "Looks like you're coming back with me."

He held onto the cat with one hand and turned the car around to go back to the Airbnb to clean up, check out, and search for answers.

***

Aaron walked out of the Dunkin Donuts with a tall dark roast and noticed a police officer come out munching on a cruller.

Aaron asked, "Excuse me officer, do you know what happened to that bookstore down the road?"

The man seemed surprised at the question. He studied Aaron for a few seconds while he ate the cruller, saliva running down his chin. He answered, "You must have just arrived from out of town. It was a fire from hell. Sirens blared throughout the night. Responders from as far away as Hyannis worked until dawn putting that damn blaze out." The cop seemed to enjoy the stunned look on Aaron's face. "Best to stay away from the place."

Aaron had a hard time swallowing. "Was anybody hurt?"

The cop stuffed the rest of the cruller in his mouth and said, "Found a fellow barbecued pretty bad. Probably a drug deal gone bad."

"How could they know that?"

"The monogrammed *N* on the gold chain around his neck pointed to a well-known local dealer. Anyhow, stay away from the place. If a fire hadn't burnt it down, a bad storm would have destroyed it. Been boarded up for the last couple of years."

Aaron dropped his coffee. The cop was already

walking back to the cruiser before he could say he anything. Jennie paced back and forth on the dashboard, visibly upset with the encounter.

He ran back to the car. "Let's get out of here." Aaron's hand shook as he spoke to the cat.

Back on Route 6, he leaned forward against the steering wheel, as if willing the Toyota to go faster. The early morning sunshine had been replaced by gray clouds moving in from the ocean. As they passed a sign for the turn off to the White Cedar Swamp Trail in Wellfleet, a low-level fog rolled in over the road.

Then it happened.

A dog appeared in the middle of the road. He hit the brakes. Jennie dropped to the floor. The car fishtailed before it came to a sudden stop. It was a Rottweiler. The dog sauntered over to the car and stood up on its hind legs, pressed against the driver's window.

Face to face with Aaron, it bared its teeth, its eyes a brilliant red. It gave no bark, but a deep growl that filled the inside of the car with a preternatural sound.

Jennie jumped back onto Aaron's lap. Her fur stood on edge and her eyes shimmered a bright green.

The dog and the cat glowered at each other. Aaron sat frozen in his seat, powerless to move or comprehend what was unfolding.

Finally, the dog backed off. It swung its head away, sending saliva flying through the air. It galloped across the fog-covered road and vanished into the white cedar forest.

In a half trance, Aaron started the engine again and righted the car with Jennie back on his lap. He floored the Toyota, cutting a swath through the fog. His heart raced and his mind spun around, wondering what kind of story needed to be told.

Ghosted
Jan Cronos

unrequited
no reply to his text
wimpy emoticons of love
just nada, stark indifference as if
he's nought, non-existent
a spectre or less and now
when he tries to call her
his fingers are breezy
feeling unwell they
gust like vapors
pass right through his cell

A Portrait Of Death in Grief & Brief
A. A. Alhaji

my father's portrait lies on the oak table,
the hyperbole around it are memories
of his wisdom on death & its brief spell
and what remains of a birth after eternity
is a crust of bones lying beneath graves
around corners, with the same smell of
sunflowers hushing the dead ponies
a funeral silence hangs out with the sunset
carving a symphony of a century immortal
only to God. helplessly, i watched my mother's
tears fall in the vase that once
held my father's ashes.

"Ectoplasm" by Hira Rashid

Trans-Allegheny Lunatic Asylum
Lee Clark Zumpe

Drowning in senseless delirium,
wasted to shadow and bone,
a tragedy of disposition and situation –
locked in cages, lobotomized,
ostracized and tortured;
waiting for their grave clothes –
to accompany those fortunate souls
who have already gone, mercifully,
to their long homes –
no memorial to mark their passing,
no headstone, no obituary,
shunned, banished, and forgotten –
now inclined to endless repetition,
mustered for eternity
in spectral vigilance.

Photo credit: The Travel Channel

Aveline's Apartment
Shikhar Dixit

Aveline dropped her backpack and purse on the floor, locked her apartment door, and collapsed onto the sofa. She kicked off her shoes, put her feet up on the coffee table, and cast a long, loud sigh into the dim living room.

The new living room. She spent all night moving in, then had to rush off to work this morning on no sleep. After eight grueling hours in the restaurant, she went to her night class. She endured three more hours of *Abnormal Psychology* lectures, before she could return to her new home. A month had passed since she left Phil (the cheating skunk!). After crashing with her parents, she managed to find this apartment, surprisingly cheap for such a nice place, and with the help of Dad and Uncle Harry, she finally moved in.

Aveline managed a moment of genuine contentment. This place was hers and hers alone.

She dreaded having to whip up something for dinner. Aveline heaved herself to her feet and was headed for the kitchen when the doorbell chimed.

Dropping her head, Aveline just stood limp for a moment. What now?

She spun on her stockinged heel and opened the door. An older woman holding a pie greeted her. She was slight of build with short-cropped gray hair, and bottle-thick glasses that magnified her eyes to comically tremendous proportions.

"Hello," she said a bit loudly, "forgive me if I'm calling at a bad time. I'm Bernice Shiloh...your neighbor!"

Aveline took a tremulous step back from the woman's sheer volume. "Hi," she replied. "Nice to meet you. I'm Aveline."

Bernice craned her neck sideways, around Aveline's shoulder, as if trying to get a glance inside the apartment. "I brought you some Boston Cream," she continued loudly, then added in a more reasonable volume, "you know — for housewarming." Bernice shoved the pie into Aveline's hands.

"Oh, thank you," she managed, then, flustered she offered, "Why don't you come in?"

What am I thinking?

With Bernice now in the apartment, Aveline felt subtly trapped, as if she'd succumbed to a clever ruse. This slight, possibly deaf woman had overwhelmed her and taken charge.

"So," her mouth fluttered a moment, grasping for anything to say, "are you from 2B?"

"Where else, dear? It's just the two of us on this floor, isn't it?"

"Of course." Aveline set the pie down.

Bernice fiddled with her hearing aid.

"Sorry for the yelling, dear," now at a reasonable volume. "This old thing keeps slipping into low and I just don't notice until I've just about yelled someone's head clean off."

"No problem." Aveline relaxed a bit. Surely this was just a lonely old woman, harmless and eager for company. "Let me get a knife so I can serve us some of this delicious-looking pie. Would you like some coffee, Ms —"

"Shiloh, honey. And that's Mrs., though Henry shuffled off this mortal coil ten years ago, may God rest his soul. But you never mind that. Call me Bernice.""Coffee, Bernice?"

"Oh, heavens no. Gives me the runs."

Aveline served up two pieces of pie on the cluttered dining table and pulled up a chair for Bernice. They sat and ate quietly. Bernice stole glances around the apartment. It almost seemed as if she were searching for something. Aveline thought this was odd behavior for a complete stranger. Could she be casing the apartment for a robbery?

"I'm not looking around for nothing," Bernice offered, as if reading her mind. "I have a very good reason for coming over here, dear."

Aveline set her fork down. "You do?"

"Well, you did notice how low the rent was on this

apartment, didn't you? I mean to say, I pay nine-hundred and fifty a month next door."

Aveline's jaw dropped open. "I'm only paying six. Is your apartment bigger?"

"Same size, dear. Two bedrooms, one bath."

"Well, then why on earth ... ?

"Oh, it's really quite simple. You see, my apartment isn't haunted."

***

During the early hours of morning, weariness weighed on her bones, dragged her mind into the murky depths of sleep, but something kept her eyes open. A cautious turn of her head brought her face-to-face with the clock, which read only a few minutes past 3 a.m. She tried to figure out what had awakened her. She didn't need to pee. No knots of pre-sunrise hunger. Only the vague sense of not being alone.

The room lay heaped with shadow. Her heart beat slow but hard in her own ears. Scant moonlight filtered through the dense curtains. Too frightened to move, Aveline opened her eyes wide in the dark, hands clenched into tight fists beneath the double-layer of blankets.

Her peripheral vision jumped to follow the movement of shadows in the darkness. As her apprehension climbed, she resisted whimpering with a sheer force of will backed by fear; something might hear her and pounce. Irrationality be damned, there was something here with her. Or someone. Neither option seemed the less grievous. Maybe crazy old Bernice was right.

She considered jumping up and confronting the darkness, if for no other reason than just to put an end to this agonized cowering.

But what if that proved to be a fatal mistake? Perhaps if she stayed put, whatever lurked nearby would leave.

Of course, it made no sense to think this way. An intruder who meant her harm would harm her no matter how much she shrank, and anyone else would have noticed her presence and left.

Yet Aveline remained certain that who- or whatever it

was had not gone. It waited for her to move or sit up, or merely surveyed her bedroom, all preparatory to scaring her to death. Lying still, however, grew increasingly torturous as the seconds stretched into minutes. How long had she been like this? According to the clock, not even a minute had passed. Swallowing hard, her twisting fingers beginning to shake, she tossed the blanket back, sat up, reached over and switched on the lamp.

She screamed, flattened herself against the headboard. Her heart beat violently against her ribs, but she hadn't dropped dead yet. And for all that, she saw nothing. Starting to laugh, she slumped down, shaking her head at her foolish credulity.

But the lamp remained on as she drifted off.

**

The following day dawned low, with slate-colored clouds across the rooftops of the city. Chill air had seeped into the streets overnight. Aveline had stopped on her landing to gaze long and hard at apartment 2B before descending the stairs and heading out into that new autumn cold.

Daily, she walked to the subway, then rode for fifteen minutes. Slumped in a long, vacant seat with her backpack and purse beside her, she stared at her reflection in the dark window opposite, surveying the small dips of bruise-colored darkness beneath her eyes. She hadn't slept well.

The memory of what happened remained a vague outline until she'd reached work and was serving her first table. Then it leaped readily into her consciousness, the moments of raw terror that had pulled her out of sleep during the night, and the certainty that she'd been watched in the lightless bedroom. She only *just* managed not to drop two trays of food onto the floor.

The day crawled by, but mercifully, it was a Wednesday, which meant no class that night. She could just go back home and contemplate her empty — *haunted?* — apartment.

Her boss asked her to stay an extra two hours and Aveline found herself doing so gladly. It would delay the quiet moments she'd have to spend reintegrating with her silent abode.

As she took orders, served, even bussed her own tables, thoughts of the old woman leapt into her mind. She hadn't given Bernice much time to stay and talk after the woman's startling claim. *Aren't our elders wiser than ourselves?* Yes, but they could also be crazier, or perhaps, in the age of Alzheimer's, more addle-brained and paranoid than she knew. Bernice, however, seemed at the very least to be harmless.

Finally, Aveline left work to find the sun had managed to stab holes in the cloudy sky some distance to the west. She walked through lilac shadows, down a street strangely barren of pedestrians, rode silently on a crowded subway car, and returned to the airy streets of her own neighborhood to join the evening dimness.

When she reached the second-floor landing, she found Bernice standing outside her — Aveline's — apartment, holding a steaming casserole dish emanating the heavenliest of scents. Aveline found herself smiling as she unlocked the door and stepped into the shadowy confines. She flicked on the living room light and held the door for Bernice.

"Tuna casserole," the old woman offered as Aveline set about clearing the dining table and putting out dishes, almost as if she'd never left the restaurant.

"Smells good," she said as she pulled out a chair for Bernice.

"It's elbow macaroni, cheddar cheese, Bumblebee Tuna, and breadcrumbs."

They cut squares in an absurdly comfortable silence, and dug in with forks. The hiss of the apartment heaters kicking on, footsteps from various parts above and below Aveline's apartment, and occasional traffic sounds provided background music for the meal. It wasn't like any kind of meal she'd had before. Her parents, her ex-boyfriend, all her family, were a gaggle of talkers for whom eating was a social affair.

It was nice, until the moment came for Bernice to set down her fork and ask, "Well? Anything?"

Aveline began shaking her head immediately.

"I heard you scream," said Bernice. "I'm usually up in the middle of the night."

"It was nothing. I spooked myself."

"Surely, child —"

"I didn't see a thing," Aveline insisted.

"Oh. Nothing?"

Aveline sighed, wiped her mouth with a napkin, and stood up with her plate. "I think you should tell me why you think it might have been something else." She carried the dish to the sink, hoping Bernice would have nothing, no proof, no tales to tell, but her own memories of the night before zipped through her head like a mini-movie.

"The couple that lived here before you were the Cussards. Louis and Emily. They have a little boy. It was Emily who insisted something was amiss here and prompted them to move out. Not right away, of course. Oh, I could hear the arguments in the evening; Emily begging, insisting that something was bothering her in the night, that the boy, Jimmy, was having nightmares constantly, whether it was day or night. Ultimately, Louis *saw* something, but I was never able to find out what. They weren't as open to an old woman's nosiness as you are, dear.

"Prior to the Cussards — who stayed here for all of two months — there was Paul Geller, a part-time college student just like you. He *was* forthcoming about what was happening to him. He told me, Aveline, that the walls were like doors, and at night, these doors opened. He said you never knew what you were going to get, but you never got the same thing twice. Well, Paul awoke late one night to find his bed swarming with bees. He ran out of his apartment and knocked on my door. I came back in here with him and there was nothing, but he showed me the numerous stings on his body. They swelled and turned a faint orange color. By the time he was packing his things up the next day, the swelling was gone, but the little points where he'd been stung remained. I never heard from him again. I was under the impression he'd gone to live in university housing.

"And before Paul there was my friend Patricia Coleman. Patty and I were old friends. Like me, Patty had lived here for upwards of twenty years. She was only a little younger than I."

Aveline detected the slightest tremor in Bernice's hands, but the old woman's eyes remained clear, her voice matter-of-fact.

"Patricia lived alone because her husband passed away, oh, eleven, twelve years ago. One night, she called the police. She insisted that there was an intruder in her apartment. Well, the police came and searched and ultimately, they left, having found absolutely nothing but an embarrassed old woman. Another couple of weeks went by and Patricia allowed herself to forget whatever it was that had disturbed her. For my own part, I felt she'd merely had a nightmare.

"Well, perhaps two and a half weeks later, I heard her scream. The walls are thin here, Aveline, so if you ever have — mmm — male company, try and keep it down, won't you?" Bernice winked. Aveline couldn't help but turn away with a blushing smile. "So, anyway, she screamed and I hurried over. I knocked and Patty let me in. She insisted that something was in her bedroom. That was how she said it, Aveline. Not 'someone', but rather 'something.' I went into the bedroom with her, but of course, there was nothing there. I tossed her bed, even went down on these arthritic old knees and peeked beneath the bed for her. I rummaged a bit in her closet and did a thorough inspection of the rest of the house. I *even* spent the rest of the night beside her. We old biddies have to look out for one another. By the following morning, she felt foolish again, and I returned to my own apartment to finish sleeping.

"The next incident came much sooner. Only two or three days later, I don't recall exactly. I was sitting, watching some late-night television and I heard her scream again. This time, Aveline, she kept on screaming. I rushed over, knocked, and found myself knocking for some time as Patty just went on screaming, the most frightful sounds of terror I'd ever heard. I could hear her stumbling around in there, as if she were dodging an intruder. I was very frightened that she might give herself a heart attack. When, finally, the door was opened, she sprang into my arms. She said the most peculiar thing, then, as I held her up, the poor thing shivering and weeping like a child. She said, 'So many eyes.' I said to her, 'What was that, Patty?' and she said, 'I've got to stay away. I've got to stay with you, Bernice! She had so many eyes!'

"I didn't know what to think about that, but I could hear someone coming downstairs. This time, Patty's screaming had woken someone from upstairs. Well, I didn't want some question as to her fitness to live alone and so I smuggled her into my apartment and put her in my bed. She wouldn't let me leave her, but whenever I asked what she had seen, what was this about 'eyes', she would just shake her head and hold on to me tight.

"Well, Aveline, she slept like a baby in my apartment. She stayed with me for quite a few weeks. Anytime she needed something, I came over here and got it. And you know what? I got quite used to sharing the place. I found it comforting to have a roommate. We cooked together, played cards together, read aloud to one another occasionally, and of course, we watched a lot of television. It was a treat for her because she didn't have a set of her own. And I started thinking. She has no troubles as long as she's here with me. We get along wonderfully and her nightmares have stopped. Perhaps what she needed all along was company.

"So, I said to her one day, I said 'Patty? Why don't we just live here together? There's plenty of room for both our belongings — neither of us had very much stuff — and we could each spend half the amount on rent. It would be a mercy on our social security checks, wouldn't it?' Well, she started weeping, she was so happy. All we needed was to bring over her things. Her furniture could remain behind. We could arrange something with the super, if necessary. So we began to bring her things over. She entered her own apartment again, but always with me. She never came in here on her own.

"One night, we were packing a few of her things in the bedroom when I heard my telephone ring through the wall. I said, 'Patty, that could be my son,' and I left her there. God forgive me, I left her alone."

Bernice took a moment to wipe at her eyes. Aveline wanted to reach out, to comfort her, but the gesture seemed too personal with a woman she'd known for only one day. A few moments of sniffling, and Bernice continued.

"It *was* my son on the phone. He calls so seldom, you see. I talked for a good while, started filling him in on the new living arrangement. Thomas, my son, had some issues with that. I had to talk him down a bit, explain just how close Patty and I were. I was doing just that when Patricia screamed. I was a bit slower rushing over. I assumed that Patty had fallen asleep. I further assumed that she had woken in the throes of another nightmare. But in my time, I did hang up with my son and come over.

"Only, this time, Patty wouldn't let me in at all. I could hear her moving about in here, but she had stopped screaming. I knocked and knocked and kept saying to the door, 'Patty, let me in. Dammit, why won't you let me in?' I did that for nearly an hour. I became aware that there was no more noise from within. Eventually, I woke up the super and explained the situation. I had no choice. I didn't want to call the police for fear what they might do with her. Have her declared incompetent, perhaps? I didn't know. Well, the super was angry, but he came up all the same and let us in. He walked around calling, 'Mrs. Coleman! Mrs. Coleman!' I went in right behind him. We searched and found no sign of her. 'Must've gone out,' that oaf suggested.

"But I knew she had *not* gone out." Bernice closed her eyes, inclining her head in the sudden silence.

Aveline sat back, feeling strangely wrung out, as if the tale had been her own. What was she to make of all this? Should she move out over this story? According to Bernice, none of the others moved out until the situation became too much to bear. Was she to stay put and put herself through the same thing? Of course, Aveline considered the possibility that Bernice was either insane or a Class A prankster, but something about the emotion with which Bernice finished her story struck her as genuine. Beyond genuine.

"I will remain vigilant," Bernice said. "From the day I realized how amiss things were in this place, I swore I would do something about it. The super did, when he lowered the rent for this particular apartment. Well, I'll make sure I warn each and every person who steps through that door." She pointed at the entryway.

"I can't just pack up and leave," Aveline said.

"I know dear." Bernice stood up. "I think I'll head back and take a bit of a nap." She moved to the door, shuffling in a manner that made her seem her age for the first time. "Stories really take it out of me, you know. You have a good night. And if you have any problems, you know where to find me."

The door glided shut behind Bernice and Aveline truly felt the oppressive nature of the room surrounding her.

***

Bernice's tale disturbed Aveline sufficiently that she dragged her pillow and comforter from the bedroom and bunked down for the night on the living room couch. She snuggled down as comfortably as she could. Beams of amber light spilled in from the street lamp, seeping in from the edges of the closed curtains, and formed flickering bars on the ceiling. Aveline stared, trying not to think about the frightening tale of Patricia Coleman. The shadows seemed to tighten around her. She thought maybe she'd skip her class tomorrow evening. But no, that wouldn't be good. She'd miss three hours of material in one shot. There were only two more weeks left in that course. It wouldn't do to slack off now.

She yawned and closed her eyes.

Maybe if she borrowed someone's notes. There was that cute guy who sat in front of her.

An ear-shattering chirp echoed from the darkness around her. Aveline opened her eyes.

It stood on the bedroom threshold, a pair of reptilian

legs with reversed knee joints, and eye stalks growing directly out of the pelvis. Aveline screamed, tumbled out of the sofa. Huffing for breath, her feet fighting for purchase on the carpet, she managed to crawl away from it, towards the kitchen. When she finally managed to get to her feet, Aveline ran for the butcher block. She pulled the longest, sharpest knife and turned, shrieking from low in her throat.

The room stood empty. There seemed no trace of the horror she'd seen a moment ago. Gasping for breath, she walked straight out of the apartment on quivering legs and, ten seconds later, knocked on Bernice's door.

***

"Dad, I can't live here anymore."

She was answered by silence. Aveline sat in Bernice's kitchen, the phone tucked between ear and shoulder, right hand wrapped tightly around a steaming mug of coffee. She'd spent the night on Bernice's couch, despite the old woman's insistence that they share the bed. She needed the time alone so that she could quietly freak out over what she'd witnessed. During those long, nighttime hours, Aveline decided that Bernice was right. The apartment was haunted — or something like that — and she needed to get out.

As soon as she got home from work, she'd phoned Dad.

"What do you mean you can't live there anymore?"

Before she could *quite* help it, Aveline lost control and started crying. Bernice, who had been sitting nearby, stood and made herself absent. In halting, sobbing beats, she told her father the outlandish tale, the whole sordid matter, including Bernice's tale about the previous tenants. Dad took it surprisingly well.

"Okay. But it'll have to wait until Saturday, sweetheart."

"I'll stay with Bernice. We'll go over during the day, together, to get some of my things."

"Honey, are you sure about this? I mean, your mother and I will be thrilled to have you back, but are you absolutely sure?"

He didn't believe her. That much seemed obvious. But it didn't matter. She needed to get out! Aveline never wanted to see another monstrosity like the one she witnessed last night. "I'm sure, Dad. I'm telling you the truth."

"I know you're telling the truth. But isn't it possible you had some kind of ... nightmare?"

"It was real, Dad."

That seemed to satisfy him for the moment. She gave him Bernice's phone number and hung up just as Bernice came back into the room. Aveline almost laughed through her drying tears. Bernice was dressed for the day and stood with a baseball bat slung over her shoulder.

"Okay, dear. Why don't we make an expedition next door and get some of your things?"

***

That evening, Bernice prepared homemade meatballs with *farfalle* (she had no spaghetti) in meat sauce while Aveline made Parmesan and buttered toast out of stale Italian bread. They ate in companionable silence, the two of them as comfortable with each other as if they'd lived together for many years. Aveline mused on where she would move next — that is, after she returned for a short time to her parent's house. And how exactly would she clean out that horrifying apartment, wanting the entire U.S. Army in there with her and her father?

After dinner, Aveline insisted on washing the dishes. The steaming water felt good on her hands as she rinsed off the sudsy plates and silverware. Everything seemed strangely *okay*, considering what she had faced. She wondered what Bernice would do to convince the next tenants about the haunting. Maybe Aveline could help out in that regard, but she believed any prospective tenant would either consider them a couple of crackpots, or worse, a couple of liars with hidden motives for wanting the apartment empty.

As the nightly news went off the air, Bernice excused herself and went to bed.

It took Aveline longer to drift off on the couch. A vein of raw anxiety pulsed deep within her and she spent an hour talking herself down into the catacombs of sleep. There was nothing to worry about, she repeated to herself. She need never go into the apartment again.

She woke suddenly, some time near dawn, judging by the merest hint of light creeping in through the curtains. At first, only silence greeted her. She sat up on one arm, looking around Bernice's living room. Something wasn't right.

Aveline swung her feet off the couch and stumbled around barefoot, at one point knocking her toes against the coffee table. "Shit!"

Then she noticed it, the subtle difference that bothered her. Bernice's bedroom door was conspicuously open. A quick examination revealed that the room was utterly empty.

"Bernice?" Aveline called, already moving towards the front door, certain now that she knew precisely where Bernice had gone. Sure enough, the apartment door was open a crack.

"No!" Aveline rushed out into the hall and found herself knocking fiercely on her own apartment door. From inside, she could make out Bernice speaking, could even make out some of the words. One of those words chilled her.

Patty.

Aveline tried the doorknob and found that it turned easily. Pulling a deep breath, she pushed the door open and walked in. It was akin to stepping into a nightmare.

For starters, the walls were gone, replaced by an endless field of winking stars...or were those eyes? The air was wintry and Aveline could see her own breath plume in the air. "Bernice!"

She could still hear Bernice speaking to someone — or something. Her voice drifted from a space, Aveline was able to determine by using the furniture for orientation, right where the bedroom used to be. A haze of violet mist hung like drapery, separating the bedroom from everything else. The enormous sky made Aveline feel vertiginous. She bent her knees and continued on towards the bedroom with her head ducked low, afraid the sky would rip her away from solid ground.

Here and there, strange shadows darted back and forth in the darkness.

Aveline screamed more than once, ducking away from alien forms: a creature vaguely shaped like a five foot tall rabbit with reptilian skin; an even larger eight-legged arachnid whose speed was comparable to that of a cheetah; a bipedal being who, in silhouette, resembled an enormously fat man with lines incised all over his skin in such density, variety, and depth that they would never be mistaken for either tattoos or scars. She sprinted through a gap between these monstrosities, all organisms foreign to every one of her senses. At last, she reached a place where she could see through the veil.

There was no bedroom any longer. Instead, Aveline could see a steep hillside, its rocks shining with moisture and pulsing in-and-out like a stone heart. Bernice stood on this hillside, looking further up.

"Bernice! Get away from there!" But Aveline found her voice carried away on the wind. She tracked Bernice's gaze and another figure caught her attention. Further up the hill, standing in partial silhouette against a sky of whirling color, the figure of an old woman, her face full of eyes. The figure reached out to Bernice.

Aveline screamed.

Bernice reached out to the figure in return.

Aveline continued to call out, her voice growing reedy and faint. Bernice turned and looked over her shoulder. She smiled. Aveline could already see the changes this place had wrought on her face. She saw everything she needed to see and turned away, stumbling back towards the door, wherever it had gotten to.

It took a few minutes of stumbling. Something about the size of a small dog and covered in pulsating skin reared up at her at one point. Aveline yelped and reached down so she could overturn the heavy coffee table onto it. A wet crunch resounded into the endless night and Aveline finally found the doorway to the hall, to the real world. Three running steps and she launched herself through the opening. She glimpsed, just as she flew through the doorway and into the wall opposite 2A, the shadow of something massive descending on her.

She turned, her heart threatening to pound a crater into her chest, and saw the immense leonine face, framed in a black mane, running for the opening. With a supreme effort, Aveline lunged to her feet and reached through the opening. She grabbed the doorknob and pulled it shut.

The lion-analog slammed into the other side of the door with a crack like thunder.

Aveline slid down onto her haunches, back flush with the wall, and collapsed into tears.

Only the silence of early morning remained to greet her.

***

With a heavy heart, Aveline, her dad, and two burly cousins, summoned at her request, cleared out her apartment by the light of day. Dad was happy to have her home, and Aveline found commuting the short distance relatively pleasant and easy.

But she drove by the old apartment building once a week. Nobody had taken her old apartment yet. She would be watching, however.

When the time came, she would be ready to warn the new tenants.

And when they finally believed, she would be there to help them leave ...or stand and fight.

What Happened?
Denise Noe

Nobody locks a front door these days.
Jails and prisons are empty.
Attorneys, police officers, and pornographers are all looking for work.
What happened?
The devil repented.

The Walled Garden
Jean-Marie Romana

"Something there is that doesn't love a wall"
                    -Robert Frost

The garden was walled in long ago,
scraggly and untamed,
roses worm eaten, overrun with thorns.
Inside the air is still and quiet;
sounds are deadened, seasons stand still
while something waits for escape, unseen and silent.

"Standstill" by Sonali Roy

Taking Jenny Home
Sarah Cannavo

One moment the girl wasn't there; the next, there she was on the side of the road, nearly invisible in the night. Dylan Carrey might have missed her if he hadn't glimpsed her white dress glowing among the dark brush of the back road, and a moment later the yellow beams of his headlights swept across the rest of her: No jacket, despite the frost in the air, the bitter breeze stirring the short skirt of her dress around her long pale legs, a small white purse clutched tight in her left hand.

Where did she come from? Dylan wondered, feeling a pang of concern. Did she need help; had she been in an accident? He couldn't see any blood on her, and she seemed to be standing all right, but maybe she'd gone to seek help for someone who hadn't been so lucky. They were a few miles outside town, and most of these back roads were dark dirt strips, easy enough to wind up in trouble on. Every accident on this stretch raised yet another outcry to do something about it, but the small Kansas farming township was too strapped to do much, and for now those who chose not to take the main roads were offering themselves up into God's hands once the sun went down. *Can't hurt to make sure she's all right,* he figured, not liking the idea of leaving her standing there in the middle of a November night.

The girl watched the sky-blue car slow as it approached, her expression wary as she looked through the passenger window at Dylan behind the wheel. Seventeen or so, Dylan guessed, the same as him. She didn't come closer, so he rolled the window down, letting in a gust of frigid air, and asked, "You all right, miss?"

The girl gave a small smile, her cautious air relaxing somewhat. "I seem to be stranded," she said. "I let some friends of mine drag me to a party, but a couple of guys there were bothering me and I didn't feel like waiting on my friends anymore, so I left. It seemed like a good idea at the time, until I remembered I didn't have my jacket, or a ride."

"Bothering you?" Dylan asked, alarmed. "Did they... Did they hurt you or anything?"

The girl shook her head, strands of dark brown hair brushing her face light as birds' wings. "No, nothing like that. Just a couple of jocks trying to impress me and accomplishing the exact opposite. Besides, between you and me, parties in somebody's old barn aren't exactly my idea of a good time, so I was kind of looking for any excuse I could find to leave." She smiled, a white curve to match her dress, and Dylan couldn't help smiling back.

"Well, do you need a ride somewhere?" he offered. "I'm heading back into town now, and I'd be happy to drop you off."

She considered him for a few moments, taking in his tall, lean frame, the large hands loose on the steering wheel, her gaze flicking to the backseat to see if it was empty before it returned to him and she smiled again. "Thank you," she said. "I'd really appreciate that..."

"Dylan," he supplied. "Dylan Carey."

"Dylan," she repeated, as though storing the information away, and then said, "I'm Jenny Lennox."

"Hop on in, Jenny Lennox," Dylan said, popping the lock and pushing the passenger door open. "I'll get you where you're going."

It was like her appearance on the roadside all over again; he blinked and Jenny was sliding onto the cream-colored leather of the passenger seat quick and quiet as a whisper, the skirt of her dress swirling lightly with her movements like rolling mist. Her hair drifted gently around her face, hanging around her slim shoulders, and in the dim dashboard light her eyes were soft and dark, gleaming with a grateful light as she turned to him and said again, "Thank you, Dylan."

"No problem, Jenny," he said as he pulled out onto the road again, his headlights making brilliant incisions into the darkness ahead. "Where do you want me to take you?"

"Could you take me home?" she asked, for a moment sounding wistful and weary—a lost girl.

"Sure I can. Where's home?"

"Harcourt Road, the brown house at the end."

"Huh. I didn't think anybody still lived out there," Dylan said, surprised. "The last time I drove by that place it looked pretty empty to me."

Jenny nodded. "It's my mother, my little sister, and me. Mom's probably going out of her mind worrying about me; I was supposed to be home by now."

"My dad does the same thing," Dylan said, smiling faintly and fondly in remembrance. "It's just the two of us, so he worries about me a lot. Even more once I started driving. 'Be careful on those back roads, Dylan,' he always says. 'I'd rather jump in the pen with a pissed-off steer than drive down one of those at night.'" Jenny laughed at his imitation of George Carey's thicker Kansas accent, and his smile grew. She liked his smile, sweet and boyish, liked his hazel eyes, bright even in the car's dim interior, and the dimple in his chin, liked the way his brown hair fell softly over his forehead, and she was glad he was the one taking her home.

The cold was clinging stubbornly inside the car, though the heat was on; Dylan glanced over and noticed Jenny's pale bare skin was prickling with goosebumps. "Do you want to borrow my jacket, Jenny?" he asked. "It's still a little ways back to town, and I'd hate for you to be freezing the whole way there."

She smiled shyly at him. "That would be nice, Dylan, thank you." She wound the dark blue denim jacket around her shoulders, slipped her arms through the sleeves; it was a bit too big of a fit but it was warm and worn-in and comfortable, and Jenny held it tightly to her like a traveler's cloak in a fairy tale. "You have a nice car here, by the way," she added, touching the seat lightly. "I don't know much about them, but this one looks classic to me."

"Parts of it probably are," Dylan said with a crooked grin. "It's a bit of a mutt; the body's mostly Mustang, but I think there's some Challenger under the hood, and God only knows what else mixed in. I built it myself," he explained, and Jenny looked around again, eyes widening.

"*Built* it? Really?"

He nodded. "Uh-huh. I started when I was fifteen, before I could even drive. Dad owns the garage in town, so from the time I was little I was always messing around with spare parts—I found the frame in a scrap heap one day and it was in pretty good shape, but even then I was still just kinda messing around with it, you know? But the more I worked on it, scraping up more spare parts and buying them when I could, I don't know, it was like I realized maybe I actually *could* do it, get this thing running. And I did. Don't ask me how," he chuckled, "but I did. I got it inspected and everything, and it was pronounced street-legal on my sixteenth birthday." He glanced at the clock glowing in the dash, saw it was now a few minutes past midnight on a chill, dark November morning. "So I guess it's an anniversary for that now, too."

"Today's your birthday?" Jenny asked. Her white dress rustled like leaves lost in the wind as she shifted to look at him, her hair fluttering and falling soundlessly around her shoulders, and he was reminded of his she'd ghosted into his car after appearing so forlornly on the roadside, like a flickering film on the edge of fading.

"For the past three minutes, anyway," he said. "November sixteenth. It's why I was out tonight; my buddy Deke lives back there on Caldicott Road—" he gestured with his head the way he'd come—"and he and some of my other buddies wanted to get a head start on celebrating, which basically meant eating pizza and playing video games in Deke's basement until we ran out of pizza and he couldn't handle losing to me anymore."

"Sounds like fun," Jenny laughed.

"Tons," he agreed.

She unzipped her small white purse, her fingers flicking nimbly through it for a few moments before she pulled something free: a pen and a creased piece of white paper, he saw, before she smoothed the paper over her knee and went to work on it with the pen held in her left hand, blocking whatever she was doing from Dylan's view. Several quick, sure strokes, then she held it up to examine her handiwork in the dashboard light—still angling it so he couldn't see what she'd done—smiling in satisfaction before she handed it to him with a "Happy birthday, Dylan."

"You didn't have to—" he started, but her grin only grew.

"Take it," she said. "For your birthday, and for being enough of a gentleman to give me a ride home."

"Well, when you put it like that..." he said, accepting it. Her slim fingers were cold as they brushed his, startlingly so, as if beneath the skin no blood ran, but her expression was warm, sparking a glow in the core of his chest.

Up ahead there was a turn other drivers tended to whip around without regard for anyone else who might have to pass; when he had to go this way Dylan always pulled over and paused for a few moments before he reached it to make sure the coast was clear, and this time as he did he looked at what his passenger had given him. Across the top of the paper in large looping letters she'd written *HAPPY BIRTHDAY, DYLAN!* above a sketch of a slice of cake on a plate, a single candle stuck in its frosting, and below it, smaller, she'd added (*and thanks for the ride!*) ¬J

"Thanks, Jenny," he said, laying it down on the dash as he pointed the car back down the road, "really. It's great."

"You're welcome, Dylan," she said, zipping her purse closed again, and their eyes met for a moment before they fell into companionable silence. A few small drops of rain pattered on the windshield and a low lonely wind moaned through the trees that lined the road, mingling with the steady rumbling purr of the hand-built car's engine and here, on the last stretch of back road before they reached the comforting, well-lit, well-paved web of lanes that made up Elkins, Kansas, the sound seemed otherworldly, a cry from somewhere cold and empty, papered with damp dead leaves and edged with a lacework of bare spindly branches, somewhere easy to lose your way and nowhere you would want to.

But they made it into Elkins without incident, and

though the quiet of the town at night meant Dylan and Jenny could still hear the keening wind as clearly as they could on the outskirts, and though the rain had turned into a faint veil of chill mist that clung to the air and the car, it didn't seem to matter anymore. Every so often one of them would glance over at the other, and once and a while their gazes would meet and they would look quickly away, out the window or at the road ahead, smiling shyly, only to resume their looking a few moments later.

The house at the end of Harcourt Road was dark, and Dylan looked up at the windows that stared back like vacant eyes, the shadow-shrouded porch, the walkway crazed with cracks. It looked as still and empty as it had the last time he'd passed by, no sign of life within. "Well, here you are, Jenny," he said, looking from it back to her.

"Home sweet home," she agreed, a faint smile gracing her lips. "Be careful heading home, Dylan, all right?"

"I will. Thanks again for the card."

She leaned in and kissed his cheek, the barest brush of lips and tingling skin but soft and sweet all the same. "Thanks again for the ride."

They sat there smiling at each other for a moment, and then, as she gathered her bag and got out he said, "See you around, Jenny." She glanced back at him and nodded, her white dress like a stray scrap of moonlight in the dark, and as she headed up her walk her voice drifted behind her, words carried on the wind in a fading singsong: "Happy birthday, Dylan Carey."

On her porch, before she unlocked the front door, Jenny turned around to wave goodbye, but the street was empty, glistening black with a cold wet shine, and she frowned, brow furrowing. Odd that she hadn't heard him driving away on such a silent street, and that he was out of sight already; her house sat on a dead end and he would have had to turn to get out again, or at the very least reverse the way he'd come and turn once he made it off Harcourt.

She shook her head, pulling her house key from her purse. *Yep, time for bed, Jenny. You're definitely tired.*

Inside she found her mother asleep on the couch, no doubt having waited up as long as she could for Jenny to come home, the book she'd been passing the time with open on her chest. Well, that explained why the porch light wasn't on—either that or it'd burned out again, the third time in as many months, the first just days after her family had moved in to the fixer-upper her mother kept promising they'd start fixing up any day now.

Moving with the light-footed silence that had caused Ashley Lennox to nickname her eldest daughter her little cat when Jenny was young, she lifted the book from her mother's chest, closed it, and set it down gently on the end table, drawing the afghan draped on the back of the couch over her mother, who didn't stir, before scribbling a note for her—*Home safe, sorry didn't call, everything okay. Jenny*—leaving it atop the book, and slipping upstairs. Out of habit she tiptoed past her little sister's room, though Emma was sleeping over one of her new friends' house tonight, and into her own, and it was only as she started getting changed for bed that she realized she still had Dylan Carey's denim jacket on.

His father owned the garage in town, she remembered him saying. She wasn't sure where it was or what time it opened on Saturdays, but she doubted it'd be hard to find; she'd walk to Main Street later today and start the search from there. And maybe Dylan would just happen to be there, and she'd be able to return the jacket in person. Maybe even work up the nerve to ask for his number this time.

Smiling at the thought, she slung the jacket carefully over the back of her desk chair, curled up in bed beneath her blankets, and slowly drifted off to the sleep to the sound of the wind.

***

The jacket was gone.

Jenny tore her room apart and then the rest of the house in search of it, with no success. Her mother hadn't seen it when she'd come into her room that morning while Jenny was still sleeping to add the dress she'd worn the night before to the laundry, and Emma was still over her friend Kirsten's house; no chance she'd borrowed it for one of the countless costumes she was always coming up with. After several hours Jenny finally gave in and accepted that she wasn't going to find it, as upset by its disappearance as she was bewildered by it, and, dressed more sensibly this time in jeans and her own red jacket, set out to apologize for its loss and offer to replace it—not quite the conversation she'd been hoping to have with Dylan today.

Carey's Garage proved easier to find than the jacket, at least, rust-edged red letters on a white metal sign above a low blocky building just off Main Street. Attached to it was a weathered blue two-story house with a mailbox reading CAREY tilting leftward by the curb, and when she got close enough to see the *Closed—Come Back Soon!* sign hanging in the garage's front window Jenny hesitated a moment before mounting the house's front steps, noticing as she did that while an old black Ford pickup sat in the driveway, the sky-blue mutt was nowhere to be seen. She couldn't fight the brief pang of disappointment she felt then, but she could leave a message about the jacket with Dylan's dad, at least, assuming he was home.

She started to think he might not be, parked pickup or not, as the echoes of her knock died away without raising any response from within. The sky was pearl-gray above and the wind was even sharper than it had been last night, and she hunched deeper into her coat, hoping she'd finally be able to finish saving up for a car of her own soon, dreading the thought of having to walk everywhere once winter truly set in. God, what had she been *thinking* last night, walking off the way she had? Sure, the jocks had been annoying and the party not much better, but still, to rush off like that, no coat, dead phone...? She *hadn't* been thinking, that was the truth, and she'd been damn lucky Dylan had come along when he had.

In the light of day—what light there was—it crossed her mind how strange it was that she'd never seen Dylan before, not around town, certainly not in school. That smile, those eyes—no, she *definitely* would've remembered seeing that tall boy striding through the halls, leaning against a locker, filing into class. Maybe he was homeschooled and just hadn't mentioned it....

She was just about to raise her hand and knock again—there was no bell to ring—when she heard movement within, as if after some deliberation someone had finally made up their mind to answer the door. The footsteps were slow, trudging, and Jenny felt a brief stab of panic. *Oh, God, did I wake him up?* she thought, before she heard the scratch of a bolt being drawn back and the rattle of a lock being turned.

The man who opened the door was tall and broad-shouldered, but those shoulders were stooped, making him appear shorter at first glance than he was. She could see the resemblance to Dylan in the line of his jaw, the hazel of his eyes, though this man's were red-rimmed and dimmer than Dylan's and his jaw was a quilt of stubble, a patchwork of gray-tinged brown that had escaped a half-hearted attempt at shaving. He was somewhere in his late forties, she guessed, and yet seemed older than that at the same time, as if, like the cars stacked in the scrap yard behind his garage, he had been through something he wasn't meant for.

"Broke down?" he asked, wearily but not unkindly, and in Jenny's head Dylan's imitation of his father's accent rang cheerfully out—he'd gotten it dead-on. "I can give you a tow, and if it's an emergency I'll see what I can do, but if not the garage don't open again 'til Monday."

She shook her head. "No, it's nothing like that, sir. I hope I'm not bothering you; I just came by to see if Dylan was here, but his car's not. Do you know when he'll be back?"

Mr. Carey started, something flashing across his face—pain, shock, quick as a glint of moonlight on metal, and something began to gather in Jenny, a chill in the marrow of her bones November had nothing to do with. His tone was flat, forced level, as he replied, "And what might you want with my Dylan, miss?"

"He...He gave me a ride home last night," Jenny said. "I wanted to thank him again, and also apologize, because he lent me his jacket and I was going to return it today, but it was gone when I woke up and I don't know where it went. I'd like to replace it, though, if I could."

For several moments Mr. Carey only stared at her, his gaze piercing despite the redness and fog in his eyes, as if he'd spent a good long while recently crying or sleepless or both, and Jenny fought the urge to squirm under his scrutiny, wondering if she'd done something wrong by coming here, the chill of foreboding growing inside her. Eventually the older man said, "Maybe you better come in for a few minutes, miss. I think we need to talk."

After a second's hesitation Jenny followed Mr. Carey into the old blue house, her stomach tightening nervously. It had nothing to do with the man himself; she sensed no danger from him or this place. No, the worry was for Dylan, the look on his father's face when she'd mentioned him. Something had happened to him—something terrible had happened to him in the hours since he'd dropped her off on Harcourt Road. *An accident,* she thought, and horror flooded her, leaving a thick, sour taste hot on her tongue. *On his own way home he got into an accident and now he's hurt or...* She remembered the road glistening with the first drops of rain, the slick blackness of it. *We make it off the back roads all right and then he gets into an accident right here in town. Oh God, Dylan...*

His father led her to a small, living room, not dirty, just cluttered, books stacked crookedly on shelves, end tables crammed with lamps and candles that looked like they hadn't been burned in some time, an overstuffed sofa and two faded brown armchairs taking up most of the space in the room and a coffee table, its surface scratched and pocked with rings where drinks had been set down on it, claiming what was left. Across the mantel marched a line of photos of Mr. Carey, a smiling redheaded woman Jenny guessed was Dylan's mother, and Dylan himself, in one a smiling baby, dimpled even then, in another beaming as he clutched the straps of a bright yellow backpack, about to board a school bus waiting with its door open, and in another that appeared more recent working under the hood of the black pickup she'd seen out front, a smudge of dark grease on his cheek and his attention riveted on what he was doing instead of the camera aimed at him. The glass in the frames gleamed as if polished recently and frequently, reflecting Jenny and Mr. Carey as they moved through the room, Mr. Carey taking one of the brown armchairs and gesturing for her to take the other.

"So, Miss..." he started.

"Lennox," she said, noticing for the first time a bottle of whiskey, nearly empty, at the foot of his armchair and bringing her gaze quickly back to him. "Jenny Lennox, sir."

"Miss Lennox." He picked up another framed picture from the coffee table between them and handed it to her, asking. "Is this the boy you saw last night?"

It was Dylan, his bright boyish smile wide, wearing the denim jacket he'd loaned her and standing outside on a leaf-littered lawn next to his car, as recognizable as him. It was even more impressive in daylight, its body polished to a high shine, its hue the same spotless blue as the sky at the top of the shot, and Dylan's hand rested protectively on the distinctive hood. "Yes, sir, that's him," Jenny said, handing the photo back to Dylan's father. "That's his car, too—he told me he built it himself."

The ghost of a smile flickered across Mr. Carey's lined face as he looked down at the photo. "That he did. All by himself—wouldn't let me touch a tool once he knew what to do. He was damn proud of that car, and I was damn proud of him." He looked from the photo to Jenny, any trace of a smile gone. "But you couldn't have been with him last night, Miss Lennox. My boy is dead. Dylan died a year ago, in a car wreck just outside of town."

Dead.

The slow, dreamy numbness of a nightmare spread through Jenny, the sick taste of dread returning, so strong she nearly gagged. "But...But that's impossible," she said, forcing the words out through her shock. "He *drove me home* last night. I was stranded and needed a ride and then he showed up and...and he drove me back to town. He told me about his car, he...he loaned me his jacket..." The one she couldn't find this morning. "He told me it was his birthday." Her voice faltered. *This isn't possible. A year ago?* "His friends—Deke, he said, they started celebrating early..."

The mention of Dylan's friend's name seemed to jolt Mr. Carey again, and he nodded, swallowing hard. "It *was* his birthday, his seventeenth. He'd gone out the night before to Deke's house and was heading home when it happened—he wasn't drinking or anything, you understand; the coroner..." His voice cracked like thin ice under too much weight. "The coroner said Dylan's system was clean. 'Course, I didn't need no coroner's test to tell me that. My Dylan was a good boy, never woulda drank and gotten behind the wheel; I raised him better than that." Jenny nodded, and Mr. Carey cleared his throat before continuing, "He'd called me a little while before, told me he was heading home, and I told him to be careful. I don't trust those back roads, you see, Miss Lennox, never did. I always told Dylan that I'd rather—"

"—jump in a pen with a pissed-off steer than drive down one of those at night?" Jenny suggested softly.

Mr. Carey nodded slowly. "That...That's right. He was on one of those roads on his way home that night, a few miles from town. There was a couple pulled off on the shoulder; they told the police their car had broken down about ten minutes before and they couldn't get any cell reception out there, so they were trying to flag down some help, and that's when Dylan showed up. Of course he was going to try to help them; that was how he was, trying to help everybody he could—he'd give you the shirt off his back and never ask for it back."

Or his jacket, Jenny thought, feeling the warmth of it around her shoulders again, her hands curled into the sleeves.

"It was when he was pulling over that the accident happened." Mr. Carey stopped, his voice thick and unsteady, and rubbed at his face, his hand rasping against his stubble.

"He hit their car?" Jenny asked, hating herself for pressing, wanting nothing more than to stop, but needing to know what had happened to the dead boy who had driven her home.

Mr. Carey shook his head. "Black ice," he said, in the tone of someone who still couldn't believe what they were saying, no matter how many times they'd said it already. "He started to skid, according to the couple, and couldn't stop. It turned out his brakes failed, locked up on him, and his car...his car hit a tree on the side of the road. Coroner said he died instantly, that he didn't suffer. Guess that's a small mercy, but it don't change the fact that my boy's never coming home again, does it?" His hands curled into impotent fists in his lap, knuckles standing out in bony ridges beneath his taut skin. "That road, and that car. He loved that damn car, and it killed him."

Jenny sat stone-still, unable to speak, feeling as if she was made of ice and a single breath would shatter her. *No. No. NO.* This couldn't have happened, this couldn't be true. How...? But it was true grief etched in Mr. Carey's face, raw and rough in his voice, and cold hands clutched Jenny's heart and twisted as the truth sank in.

"I'm sorry, Mr. Carey," she finally forced out, the words thick in her throat. "I'm so sorry. That's...That's horrible. I..." She trailed off, shaking her head, unable to conjure up anything adequate enough.

He nodded, accepting it anyway, and then eyed her as he had in the doorway, taking her in again. "You're new in town, aren't you, Miss Lennox?"

"My family moved here at the end of August, sir."

He nodded again, looking unsurprised. "Explains why you didn't know, I guess. The accident was all people talked about for a while, but then it started to die off again, just like it always does." His voice had a bitter bite to it now, sharp as the autumn wind. "I'd hoped that maybe this would be the final straw, that maybe Dylan dying would save somebody else's son or daughter, at least, because the county would finally get off their asses and start taking care of those back roads, but it ain't happened yet, and it probably never will. There's always something more important, you see, something that has to be done first. Then it happens again and the whole thing starts right back up, like a damn wheel that just keeps turning." He sighed, anger bleeding into weariness, and rubbed his face again. "And I know his car was a part of it, that his brakes could have failed anywhere, but if... I just..." It was his turn to fall silent, his eyes filling as he looked at the photo of Dylan smiling beside the car.

"I'm sorry, Mr. Carey," Jenny repeated, her chest still tight, her head still swimming. "But I'm not lying, and I'm not crazy. Your son drove me home last night. How could... Why would he do that?"

Mr. Carey raised his eyes to her. "Because, Miss Lennox, I think he wanted you to do what he never can. I think he wanted to make sure you made it home."

***

An hour later Jenny stood in the Elkins cemetery, looking down at the plain gray stone. Mr. Carey had offered to drive her but she'd gone on her own, hoping the walk would help clear her head. She couldn't say that it had, but there was no denying the reality of the stone at her feet, its inscription still fresh and clear, not yet worn down by weather or time, its marble surface slick with the day's dampness and the same gray shade as the sky glowering above. *Dylan Sean Carey, Born November 16 1997 Died November 16 2014. Beloved Son and Friend to All.*

Thank you, Dylan, Jenny thought as she stood with her hands buried deep in her pockets and her hair stirring around her shoulders in the wind, staring down at the grave but picturing a boy with a bright smile and a fall of soft brown hair across his forehead, a boy who'd built the car that had killed him with his own two hands, hearing his soft, sweet voice, his laughter. Aloud she said softly, "Thank you for taking me home."

There was a small bouquet of flowers, frostbitten now, resting at the foot of the stone—from his father, no doubt. She wished she'd brought something to leave on the grave, some token of thanks besides a few whispered words that didn't seem anywhere near enough. A few errant snowflakes tumbled down from the clouds, small and white and easily scattered, and one touched Jenny's cheek like a kiss, melted in a moment by her heat. Something else white, more substantial than the snow, fluttered in the damp grass near the flowers—a small piece of paper, some stray bit of litter. The least she could do was pick it up, she figured, but as she did she realized that she *had* given a tribute to the dead after all, her fingers instinctively tightening on it as the wind tried to snatch it away from her and her eyes widening as she stared down at the slice of cake she'd sketched the night before, the candle stuck in it almost seeming to flicker as the paper trembled in the wind, and reread the message she'd scrawled around it.

HAPPY BIRTHDAY, DYLAN! (and thanks for the ride!) –J

For Serenity
Corrine Pridmore

The nurses had covered me up by now, far past the hope I could have been saved. I chuckled a little bit at their attempts to somehow make this better. As if Jack not being able to see the pale complexion of my face, the pasty shade of my lips, would somehow alleviate his sorrow.

There were tears in my husband's eyes as the doctor handed him our daughter. A piece of me, deep down, hated myself for tarnishing this miracle. How could I have ruined such a beautiful moment with my death?

The room was silent in the mixed moment of joy and sorrow as they let my husband celebrate our daughter and mourn my death. He hugged our daughter tight, tears dripping down his cheeks. Our daughter coughed and cried in his arms. After a moment, one of the nurses whispered, "I'm sorry." She reached out to him, expressing her desire to carry our child away.

She'd been born healthy, a miracle considering how much I'd hemorrhaged. I looked at all the red on the bed, on the floor, the blanket that draped me. I wasn't even sure when I died. One moment, Jack was holding my hand, the next, I was standing beside him as we watched people perform CPR and rush around trying to save my life. Even though I am—*was*, I reminded myself—a nurse, I simply didn't know what happened—it was just so rapid. I suppose I'd coded. Not even fast enough for a c-section.

Jack looked at the nurse in front of him with a gaze that was glossy and unfocused. I recognized this expression. Lost. Panicked. No one knew him like I did.

"Please," I said, and this word was soft. "It'll be okay. We'll manage, somehow." I reached out a hand and placed it on his shoulder. I knew he wouldn't feel it—or, at least, I figured he wouldn't. I hadn't been dead long enough to figure out the logistics of being a spirit. *A ghost*, I thought to myself.

A shiver ran up the length of his spine. I actually *felt* the slight nerve convulsions, like the after tingles of my fingers falling asleep. He almost glanced over his shoulder but seemed to think better of it, returning his gaze to the child that cried in his arms.

I bit my lip to keep from crying—*could I even cry anymore?* I couldn't help but wonder—as I looked over his shoulder to see the child I'd died for. All pink flesh with a tuft of black hair, from her father. Green eyes peeked past the scrunched-up face. Those were my eyes.

"She's beautiful," I whisper.

Jack handed our daughter to the nurse after another moment's hesitation.

"What's her name?" she asked. I leaned forward a bit, unsure of what Jack would decide. We'd barely played with names, in all honesty. After so many times of trying and burying our children, it had become too painful to imagine the could-be families we lost and what they could have been named.

He paused, weighing our options. "Serenity Marie."

I smiled. Serenity. God, I loved that name. He'd never cared for it. Marie was my name. The nurse nodded and took our daughter from him. Another nurse placed a gentle hand on his shoulder and led him from the room. I followed them out. Away from my body. Away from my death.

***

"Jack, I wish you wouldn't take our child into that God forsaken house," I said. As usual, he didn't respond, didn't react. He got out of the car and walked around so he could grab Serenity's car seat.

I stayed still for a moment, not quite sure why I was sticking around.

It was a question, the question of the moment I suppose. Where was heaven? I doubted I'd been evil enough to go to hell, but where were those damn pearly gates? Did I have unfinished business? If I did, how did I finish it? I'd never even had the option to choose. Watching my husband force a smile as he greeted my family and our friends for the funeral while he cries himself to sleep every night was...*awful*...

He's so alone, and I can't help him. This helplessness. This must be my hell. A few tears inched down my face.

I'd found out two weeks ago that the dead could cry.

I didn't bother trying to open the car door as I stepped from the vehicle. The longer I stayed dead, the less I try to act alive. I don't try to open doors anymore, though I can feel their substance. Being a ghost isn't how Hollywood portrays it. My body passes through things, but I can *feel*. Like warmth and movement, much more acutely than I could when I was alive.

"Jack, I hate this house. I wish you would just move. I wish we had moved the first time I said something about it." I hurried to keep up with his stride. The house loomed, a brick monstrosity of a two story. The brick was crumbling at the corners, the roof missing tiles. A fixer-upper, he'd called it. *Cheap, Marie, and we can make it ours! We can have our own dream house to raise our family.* It's funny now. Just as we'd almost given up on a family, we'd certainly given up on fixing up an unfinished ancient house. He'd slowly started rebuilding when I'd shown no signs of miscarrying after my second trimester, but I doubt that he would ever be able to rebuild now. He needed to move to something he could manage on his own —but, my Jack was stubborn at the best of times.

Ivy grew up on the worn-out porch that creaked as he stepped up. The heavy oak door with faded red paint groaned in protest of being opened. The hallway was old and tired, and sunlight had never reached its farthest corners.

Jack sighed and rubbed his brow. He picked Serenity up out of the car seat and hummed a song to her as he made his way to the kitchen. He prepared her bottle. "The itsy-bitsy spider crawled up the water spout…"

"Down came the water and washed the spider out," I muttered. I shook my head and walked up the stairs to our bedroom. Sometimes it was too difficult to watch him feed our daughter, knowing I would never hold her as my own.

I laid back on our bed with a small sigh, watching the walls of the house contort with a constant heartbeat. Something about the house, something about the whispers I heard at all times made me fearful. I don't know if being dead made me see things differently or if there was something...*different*...about this house. I never felt like I was *alone*. Though I knew no eyes could see me, I always felt watched. Like I was weighed on someone else's scales. I don't know if I hallucinated, but something deep within me told me I didn't. It seemed that *something* was in this house, perhaps waiting just for me. I'd felt it when I was alive too, but Jack had dismissed my concerns, saying that I was letting the old house get to my head.

I wonder what he would say now, if he could see what I saw.

I saw shadows now, out of the corner of my eye. Things moved, in an intentional and sentient way. If Jack had noticed, he'd said nothing. At least, aloud where I could hear him. Since he'd returned from the hospital with Serenity, the air in the home had changed. It made me uncomfortable. It was a building aura of anger and lust that made the walls shudder in a sick sort of expectancy.

Jack's footsteps on the stairs broke me from my troubled thoughts and I ignored the shifting walls of the house like I had for the last two weeks. I heard him rustle in Serenity's bedroom, putting her to bed.

"I love you, Marie," he said, closing the door.

I stayed silent, watching him walk in and undress in his night clothes. Something stirred inside me, a longing for comfort that I know will never be mine again. As Jack laid down beside me, the tears started once more.

"Jack, I wish I could help you," I said to him, and I put a hand on his shoulder.

His spine shivered and his eyes flicked to where I lay, almost meeting my eyes. Wild moments like this make me wonder if one day we could see each other. He reached over and pulled my pillow to him, hugging it and breathing into it deeply. I knew that he would cry himself to sleep. I couldn't watch it. Not again, and the dead do not sleep.

I left.

I knew something was wrong immediately when I entered the hallway. The narrow hall seemed darker tonight, more sinister. The walls groaned and moaned, seeping with a malicious intent. I wrapped my arms around me as I watched the ceiling sink in a deep breath.

"Get out, get out. She's mine...mine...mine...mine..."

I'd never heard a voice quite like that. Broken and sad, but firm, and terrifying. Full of lust. Feminine. Young and deadly. If I had had a heartbeat, it would have paused at the pain twisted into the words.

"Who are you?" I demanded. I'd been hearing whispers since I'd died, but this was the first time I'd been able to understand them, and the cruelty scared me. "What are you doing here?"

"Get out. Get. Out. You are not welcome in my home. She's mine...mine...mine...mine."

"Who's yours? This is *my* house..." my voice paused as I caught movement at the edge of the hall. A shadow detached itself from the corner and scuttled in a broken, haphazard movement toward the door at the edge of the stairway. Serenity's bedroom. I stepped closer, close enough to see a glimpse of a long, pale dress, of gray skin and tattered lace. Long legs seemed to rise from the figure in arching gateways, clacking and scratching against the ceiling and the walls.

She looked at me, and the pain and anger were enough to make me stagger. She wore the emotions as power, manifested and *real*.

"No..." I watched the monstrosity of legs, blackness and lace meld into the walls. She inched her way into the door of my daughter's bedroom, leaving a stench of mold and rot and roses. The walls around me convulsed with her power. I pounded at the door, surprised I could no longer pass through it.

"No! Let me in! You can't have her. You can't have her!" I pounded and screamed and for once the door shook beneath my touch. "Serenity! *Serenity!*"

My baby started to cry, and I could hear someone crooning to her *"The itsy-bbitsy spider..."*

"Oh God..." I backed away as I watched hundreds... thousands...of spiders dart from beneath the door. Thousands of bodies with long legs and cruel pincers.

I ran toward Jack's room and passed through the door, screaming. He remained passive and unaware.

Please, God. I never asked you for anything, but please... I reached out to touch my husband's shoulder and passed through.

I screamed in frustration and my voice shook the walls around me. Jack frowned and turned over.

He almost heard me, I thought. *It's emotion, it must be.* The spirit that was with my daughter. Whatever had happened to her to turn her into what she was now, there was so much pain and betrayal. She wore those emotions as weapons, and the whole world had bent to her will.

I thought of our daughter. I thought about all my resentment of dying before I could raise my family, of my guilt for leaving Jack alone to deal with this world. I thought of my anger at the spirit for touching what was mine.

A mirror shattered and Jack's eyes opened, inches from my own. The world seemed to pause as his eyes focused on my face. There was a moment of confusion—a moment where he smiled before he remembered that he'd buried me—before his mouth opened in a scream.

"No, no, Jack. Listen to me. Get our daughter. Something's got her. Something's..." I could tell that an explanation was going to be useless. "Our daughter, Jack! *Now!*"

He sprung from the bed and ran, jerking the door open and going down the hall where the walls contorted and squeezed in the spirit's anger. The fear in his eyes told me that he could now see all the supernatural energy forcing its way through the house as I followed. We stopped at the edge of the wide pool of spiders. They crawled over each other in a swirling mass. Serenity cried in her room. I wondered if he could hear the singing like I could. Something told me that he could. He looked over his shoulder, looking for me. His eyes passed over me and he couldn't see.

"Marie?" He looked away and back toward the roiling expanse of arachnids. Serenity's cries stopped in mid-breath, and I watched the blood drain from his face. "Serenity!"

There was no hesitation as he pushed forward and I watched the creatures tear at his feet and hands, crushed and biting. He winced and cried out but kept forward as he shoved his shoulder against the oak door. He tried once more, and the door did not budge.

All at once, I felt the spirit's power leave the world. The walls ceased groaning inward, and the spiders were gone. Jack's shoulder gave in and he stumbled as the door opened. For a moment we were still until Jack struggled to his feet and limped to her crib.

"She's gone." The words were broken, the voice hollow and terrified. "Marie...Marie! Are you here? God, I'm going crazy. My daughter...not her too. *Not her too.*" He dropped to his knees, burying his face into his hands. His voice shook in ragged sobs. Ugly blotches and knots marred his legs and arms where the spiders had gnawed.

"The basement." I remembered the smell around the figure. Jack had begun digging and finishing the basement a few months before I'd gotten pregnant and stopped when he'd prepared Serenity's room. The must and rot of the dirt from the unfinished basement was what I had smelled around the spirit. "Jack, the basement."

He didn't hear me. I put a hand on his shoulder, feeling the convulsions of nerves travel up his arm. He looked up, his eyes almost meeting mine. I tried to tug his shirt, begging him without words to follow me. I pulled harder, almost catching the edge of the material. He stood with difficulty.

"I'll follow, Marie. I'll follow."

I almost laughed in the manic relief that I felt. I kept concentrating and yanking on his shirt. He caught on quickly and followed me down the stairs and into the basement.

Serenity's cries answered us, and I breathed a sigh

of relief as Jack ran down the stairs.

"Serenity?" Jack's desperate plea speared another quill of fear through my heart. Where was our baby? If we could hear her? A strange, deep and vertigo inducing horror filled me as I heard Jack begin to tear at the dirt with the shovel. I ran down the stairs to see him desperately digging. The moist clogs smelled of death. He dug for almost half an hour.

"I'm sorry, Marie...Oh God. I'm so sorry." He sobbed as he dug, repeating the words over and over. I wasn't sure if he was talking to me or our daughter.

His shovel struck something solid.

Jack stumbled to his knees and clutched at the dirt with his fingertips. Wood showed beneath the dirt, showing the door of a rough, crudely made coffin.

"Oh..." I covered my mouth with a hand as Jack jerked the door open.

She lay there, clutching our child in a loving embrace. It was sad, how gently she cradled the sleeping and safe baby. What was left of the body's hair laid out behind her in a rotting halo. A knife stuck cruelly from her chest, just above where Serenity slept. Spiders tumbled over each other from a mouth that voiced a silent scream, and none touched Serenity.

"How do I get her without...?"

I finally understood it all. Why I was there. Why I hadn't moved on. This had always meant to pass. I blinked the tears from my eyes and smiled a soft smile.

"Jack."

His eyes widened at my voice, and he looked behind him, his eyes locking onto mine. "Marie?"

"I'm sorry. I never meant to leave you on your own. I love you."

"What's..."

I shook my head. "This home will never be safe for you or her to ever be able to enter again. Have others come for your stuff. Don't come looking for me. I won't be here."

Jack reached a hand out to try to touch me but I shook my head. "Keep her safe for me, Jack." I was crying now, tears dripping down my face. "You're going to be a wonderful father."

A painful understanding crossed his expression. "I love you, Marie."

"I'm so glad I got to tell you goodbye, Jack," I whispered. "Grab Serenity and run. Don't look behind you and don't stop to grab anything. Just run. I won't be able to hold her back long."

He nodded and reached out for Serenity. The walls began to shudder and build in whispers. "Hurry."

He picked up the sleeping child and the spiders began to spew from the corpse's mouth, reaching out as a corporeal force toward Jack.

"*Run!*" I screamed the word. He looked at me, eyes pleading and lost. A pain so intense that I doubt it would ever completely leave his eyes. He didn't hesitate as he broke the gaze and hugged Serenity to his chest, bolting up the stairs.

Anger and remorse inched their way through the air, originating from the body. I let my own sorrow meet the emotion and reached my arms out toward the body. "They're mine. Serenity's *mine*."

"*Mine...mine...mine...mine...*"

The spirit seeped out of the walls facing me in pale lace, black legs and malice. Empty eyes regarded me with a painfully pure hatred. I heard the front door slam, and I knew that Jack and Serenity were safe.

I smiled through my tears.

The walls groaned and the ceiling shook above us, shaking down particles of dirt, wood and dust as my emotions melded with the older spirit in front of me. I raised my arms, feeling the power contort around me, facing the clicking embrace of the jilted soul. Despite the sadness around me, despite the anger that resounded in the depths of me, there was a tranquility within me. I was that calm to the spirit's storm. My business was complete, and I could move on. Finally, I was at peace in my sorrow, knowing I've done it all for Serenity.

DRUDE
Herika R. Raymer

Lana's eyes welled as she gazed out the back window to the empty sandbox, where a memory of her daughter, Leigh Anne, played. The mental images overlaid the empty reality in front of her. Echoes of child-like laughter tormented her.

"You need to eat."

She did not move. Physical hunger did not bother her, but the heartache plagued her. She needed to hear her daughter's voice again. She needed Dead Ringer. Unfortunately, the number was disconnected.

"Sweetheart, please." Her husband knelt beside her and placed a warm hand on her cool arm. "You've barely eaten since you got home. The doctor said you needed to keep your strength up."

'What's the point?' she asked herself. Survivor's guilt cloaked her in its suffocating embrace. 'Why take my baby and leave me behind?' The question rattled in her brain constantly.

Her spouse sighed. "The doctor recommended a psychiatrist."

Lana's head snapped towards him.

His sad eyes met her blazing ones. "I miss her too, love. But the accident happened almost a year ago. I'm sorry it happened, but it's not your fault."

She could not believe him. As if there were a time limit on her sorrow and guilt! He did not understand. Dead Ringer did. He helped her to talk to her baby. She did not need a head doctor, she needed to hear her daughter's voice. She just had to find him again!

"Lana, please..."

She rose abruptly from her chair and shook off his arm. A desperate need to find the one person who could ease the pain flared. He was still in town, he had to be.

She would find him.

***

Etienne Laurent sat in R. Leig's hotel room while he

considered the Hunter's words.

The Locator's most recent assignment, to track down a World War II toy phone which supposedly allowed individuals to talk to the dead, found him in Huntsville. He tracked enough items to know such things were highly unlikely. Not impossible, but unlikely. More than likely something more sinister was involved, which was why it was fortunate Leig was there. Actually, it was his friend Caz's foresight. The ex-occultist helped Laurent on a couple of jobs, and he trusted the other's instincts about impending trouble. After the encounter in Maple Hill Cemetery, Laurent had no wish to repeat any mishaps - especially life threatening ones.

"So, you saw it, didya son?" the older man asked needlessly.

Laurent's pallor provided the answer. Just the vague memory of it prompted the Locator to leave Huntsville. He had no desire to tackle with it again.

"Describe it."

The Locator shifted uncomfortably.

The Hunter's eyes were intent on his guest as he waited.

"A shape, black as pitch." He began slowly. "Even in the dark, I could see it on his shoulders. I-It hissed at him when it realized I could see it. Sounded snake-like."

The older man leaned forward at that detail. "What'd it say?."

He swallowed dryly. "Told Dead Ringer I could see it, and was not pleased when I refused to approach. Said something about me 'resisting temptation'."

"The response?"

"That since I paid, it should be good for something."

The veteran's brows rose.

"Something about 'a few days'."

The older man's fingers tapped restlessly before he sat back. "So that's what they messed with."

Laurent's brow furrowed. "What?"

"The girl you talked to. Said her friends met with Dead Ringer a few months back."

The Locator rubbed his forehead. "Yeah. I

suspected it was the reason her friend ended up in the hospital."

"And you still set up the meeting without protection." The other pointed out.

He shrugged. "Cursed objects have a perimeter, usually not too big. Thus far, the worst happens with physical contact." He said the latter with more bitterness than he intended.

The Hunter smirked. "Learn the hard way?"

Laurent began to shut down. However, it was not the Puritan funeral item he re-lived. Instead Natalie's memory pushed forth, along with the pain. That creature knew the exact lure.

The Hunter frowned and muttered something.

"What'd it mean?" Laurent asked. "I understand it meant to feed off me, probably how it fed off the women earlier. But 'resisted temptation'?" He did not voice his suspicion of what it hinted at. It meant the man was not peddling dreams or illusions. The item was not only real and cursed, but had an active entity attached to it. It meant Caz was correct to contact a Hunter, because Laurent was absolutely in over his head. He glanced at the older man.

Leig's eyes were on him, but were distant. The Locator recognized the look as the other mentally reviewed information. After a few minutes, he spoke. "You know what you got, doncha?"

He remained silent.

"Drude."

"Druid?"

Leig coughed a laugh. "No, son. Older than that. Drude. D-r-u-D-E. Nasty things. Feed off people."

'So, I was right. Great.' Laurent thought grimly. With a name, he reviewed his internal library. Drude. European. Old Lore. Creature that fed off dreams. He frowned. What the hell was it doing here? He shook off the ridiculous question. Entities had places they preferred, but like any predator they would move to where more accessible prey resided. The creature must have ridden someone from Europe to the States. Yet something did not add up. He reviewed what little information he had, it was nothing like what he experienced "How do you know? I mean, don't those feed from dreams?"

The older man sat back in his chair and reached over to the night stand. The younger man watched him pick up a pipe, a small pouch, and a multitool. He opened the pouch and a pleasant aroma emitted from it as he shook it.

"Reality is never like myths or legends," he took a pinch and put it in the pipe bowl, "but they always contain a grain of truth. The victim needs to be in a dream-like state for Druden to feed off their life. The longer they feed, the weaker their prey after."

That made sense. Yet how did the Druden get someone to stay put? Granted, people become deaf to their instincts thanks to the worship of science. Still, there were always warnings even the most ignorant could not ignore. "But how...?"

"My guess? That toy is a lure. The promise of contact with a dead loved one is mighty powerful. Makes people ignore the most blatant of signs." His eyes cut to Laurent. "I'm sure you smelled it."

It took a moment for him to understand, but then he grimaced.

Leig nodded. "Rotten eggs. Sulfur. Usually denotes the presence of a demon."

"Must be why Dead Ringer wears heavy cologne. To cover the smell."

"Makes sense." Experienced fingers worked with the pipe. "Bring a target in with the lure, hide or cloak any warnings, and then wait for prey to submit to temptation."

Laurent digested this. "You mentioned 'temptation', like it did. Why is that important?"

The veteran snorted. "Dead Ringer, as you call him, made a pact with the demon. Lives in exchange for loot. For demons, it's easier to feed when the target is vulnerable. Provide temptation to lower their guard. When they accept the offer, they don't protect themselves like they should, which allows for an opening. The demon takes advantage of this and siphons what it wants." The veteran tamped down the tobacco. He reached over to open the window beside him, and then lit the pipe. The pleasant woodsy scent filled the room. The older man chuckled at the astonished look on Laurent's face. "Boy, I've been smoking a pipe for longer than you've been born. Ain't no way I'm allowing stupid regulations to take away my pleasure. Although, as a point of manners, I do my part to find like-minded motels and such. There are still a few, mind you. Only a few. Hard to locate. They don't want to advertise, of course."

Laurent frowned but recognized there were more important issues to address.

Leig shrugged and continued. "The demon won't kill them, not part of the bargain. Can't have repeat customers if that happens. Also, it puts the Druden on our radar to track it down for a permanent solution. So, it simply snacks. The toy pulls in lives flavored with grief, the demon provides the illusion, and when they believe they're talking to a loved one it draws them into a kind of fugue-state so it can feed. The longer they talk with their 'loved one', the more energy it takes from them."

"So it manipulates the memory."

The Hunter smirked at him. "Yes, indeedy." He nodded, inhaled, and blew out a stream of pleasant smelling smoke. "Memories. Dreams. They're similar, but different. After all, you revisit loved ones, past and present, in dreams. Some claim to see people they've never met in dreams, only to encounter them later in life." He chuckled. "Funny thing, the mind. Capable of so much, and we still don't know a fraction of what it can do."

"But the Drude does."

"Oh yes." He shook his head and took another long puff. "So, what'd you plan to do?"

"About?"

"Getting the toy."

"Well," the Locator hedged. "I need to get it away from Dead Ringer."

"Ayup, but you know he ain't about to let it go. Neither will the Drude powering it."

Laurent's mind worked fervently. "Everyone... uh,

everything has a weakness. The demon obviously knows how to manipulate its targets, but there's got to be a way to lure it and deal with it."

The Hunter puffed on his pipe, his expression stoic. The Locator was not completely certain, but it seemed the older man knew what was needed. His gut told him the solution was unpleasant, and that was why the old man did not answer immediately.

Leig took a deep breath, put the pipe on a stand seated on the table, and made his way to the dresser. Laurent watched as the older man picked up his cell phone to make a call. He did not look pleased as he waited for the other party to answer.

"Yeah." He greeted the person when they picked up. "Need ya, Burnes." The Locator could hear a male voice but could not make out the words. "Then send your protégé." Another response. "Can it, Burnes! You got McKinlee with ya. I got a Drude here. I need backup." There was a long pause. Leig sighed deeply. "I realize you'd rather be with him, but it's not like I'd reach out if I thought I could deal with the thing alone," he rubbed his neck, "and to be honest his youth will be an asset in this case."

An angry response met that. Laurent wasn't sure if he should be insulted by the Hunter calling in another one of his ilk to help. Then again, Caz directed Leig to him for a reason. This was more his territory.

"Don't give me that!" Leig barked. "We're Called, and all jobs are part of the training. You can't coddle that boy forever."

If the veteran wanted more help, he undoubtedly needed it. It irked the Locator that his presence was not enough. To be fair, he was terrified of the Drude and dreaded an encounter with it again. This reaction was undoubtedly why the other man wanted another Hunter. Laurent did not want to think about what kind of creatures the Hunters dealt with that made them so resilient.

"I'll return him to ya in one piece," Leig concluded before he hung up.

Laurent grimaced and attempted to stand. His body protested at the motion with a wave of nausea that almost knocked him over. He managed to stay upright, and gingerly made his way to the window. Oddly, the pipe scent helped focus his senses while the sunlight warmed his eerily cool skin. The longer he stood by the window, the better he felt.

"Good."

His eyes darted to the older man.

"Appears the Drude didn't take too much from ya, if you're able to move and walk."

"Why doesn't that sound encouraging?" Laurent thought bitterly.

"Now," Leig grunted as he resumed his seat and his smoke, "you're gonna use your skills to track down 'Dead Ringer' again."

The Locator stared at him.

"Once you've done that, you'll entice him into another meeting. This needs to be done before that thing spurs the idiot to leave town. My presence prompts them both to lay low for a bit, but greed will lure them to the open. Help will arrive in three days, tops. In that time, find the pair and make the arrangements. Leave the rest to us."

"It'll be in the playground again."

Leig shrugged. "We'll use it as a home advantage. Their hubris will work for us." The older man sucked in on the pipe, and then exhaled another long stream of pleasant smelling smoke. "Just don't give in to temptation, and don't run."

The young man gaped at his host.

"It knows your weakness now. That makes you a tasty morsel, easy to lure. It won't waste time with pleasantries next time. It already knows you."

His eyes roved back to the window. " 'A few days worth'," he quoted.

The older man nodded. "I've been careful to not be seen around you too much, hopefully it won't make a connection between us."

"What about the man?"

Leig scoffed. "He'll be more interested in the payout. The Drude's survival demands it pay attention to other details."

"It saw you rescue me, right?"

The Hunter shook his head. "It fled from the Authority trusted in me."

Laurent regarded him, puzzled.

"It will know my... 'taste'. That's why I called for help. When it's time to meet, we'll be close and deal with the Drude. But I can't be too close while you search for the thing."

The young man ran a shaky hand through his hair in agitation. This toy was more trouble than anticipated. Not for the first time, he wondered why he accepted an assignment from the Collector. He wondered if she intentionally sent him on this dangerous task. The last few jobs from her were progressively more hazardous. He should be able to track and retrieve an item solo with proper prep. With the exception of the Aztalan incident, at each task he got injured. It was painfully apparent he needed to re-evaluate his association with the Collector. He liked a challenge, but he was not such a thrill seeker that he was blind to the potentially fatal implications from a continued association.

"Hey, boy."

He turned to the gravelly voice. Leig continued to puff while he gestured to the dresser. Laurent crossed the room and was not surprised to see his phone, wallet, keys, and other personal items laid out.

"Best return to your hotel."

Laurent nodded mutely as he pocketed his belongings.

"Keep me in the loop."

He surmised the older man already input his contact information. "Let me know when your friend arrives."

Bushy eyebrows shot up and the veteran chuckled roughly. He muttered something illegible around the stem of the pipe. After he took another deep inhale and blew out a thick stream of aromatic smoke.

Laurent blinked. "Didn't catch that."

Leig grinned. "Yeah, keep your eyes open."

"For what?"

Another rough chuckle, but the Hunter was done answering questions. Instead, he reached into his collar and pulled out something. A circular silver insignia dangled from the short chain. The Hunter tapped the insignia three times.

Laurent blinked in surprise. His eyes zeroed onto the symbol etched into the smooth surface. It was peculiar. From a distance, it appeared like a strange upright 'S' with a circle in the middle. He committed the image to memory before he left.

***

Lana sat on the dilapidated slide of Dead Children's Playground, a small stylized duck plushie in her hands. Her empty gaze stared at nothing as her fingers caressed the toy. Her mind turned over the recent events as she pondered her next move.

Dead Ringer was a ghost. All the previous information, numbers, and locations to contact him were defunct. Her only link to talk to her daughter had slipped through her fingers! It was not fair! Her child was taken from her too soon. She found solace in her baby's voice.

Lana never considered paranormal matters, and any opinion before Dead Ringer would be of doubt. She had personal beliefs, fueled by childhood religious teachings, but in adulthood a lot of things became gray. Especially when survival went from paycheck to paycheck. The monotony was broken when she got pregnant. Termination was considered, mostly due to financial concerns. However, bottom line, Lana could not extinguish the life within her. Once she held her precious baby girl, joy vanquished all doubt. Everything had meaning. Daily struggles were still hard, but a home filled with her child's laughter was the reward. Lana swore Leah Anne helped her rediscover the wonder of everyday life.

Through her daughter's eyes, she rediscovered the beauty of sunlight bursting through treetops, the serenity of driving down a tree-lined street as their branches embraced overhead, of the laughter of water from a anything from a brook to the ocean waves, the different voices of animals as they talked to one another, and so much more. It was incredible how innocent and how simple a child's mind was. Yes, she heard and read about how some were born bad, but Leah Anne was not. She was a darling. Her compassion, even at such a young age, astounded her. Her favorite hobby was learning about animals, and she adored going to feeding farms and lakes where people could feed fish or, especially, ducks. Her most cherished memory replayed the trip to Memphis to see the Peabody Ducks.

"Mommy! Mommy! Look! Are they duck royalty?"

Lana smiled as she recalled how her daughter jumped and pointed to the procession of the ducks when they entered the door and followed the red carpet to their destination. She initially thought the event was silly, yet Leah Anne insisted on seeing it. In fact, the plush toy in her hands was from that day. It was Leah Anne's treasured possession. Her baby took it with her everywhere. It never left her hands for long.

Leah Anne still clutched it when the rescuers pulled her limp body from the mangled car after the drunk driver hit them.

A sob erupted from Lana as she clutched the toy to her chest.

"My baby…"

A familiar aroma drifted forward. An intense cologne covered another unpleasant scent which prompted her gorge to rise. Her eyes eagerly searched the abandoned playground as she unconsciously suppressed the gag reflex.

"Welcome, Lady," the smarmy voice greeted her. "We have business?"

Lana gazed longingly at Dead Ringer with a tremulous smile. When he returned the smile, she misread the predatory gesture. All the bereaved mother could see was the means to hear a cherished voice. She had no money to offer, but she would find a way to make good on this chance now that it was granted to her.

***

Dallas Charl must leave Huntington. His 'friend's agitation was infectious. Usually, when Samhain approached, its gleeful antics showed how it eagerly anticipated the buffet which inevitably occurred. However, this time it's edginess also made him uneasy.

The buffet must be brought forward to obtain enough energy for it to last until they relocated.

Charl knew this woman had no money, so he would propose an alternative. An affordable discount which a group of friends of hers could contribute to, and he would allow each one some time on the phone. The group would provide funds and food.

After which, he would leave their unconscious forms and Huntington behind.

***

Etienne Laurent reviewed his notes while he stood in line at Yolo Rollo. He ignored the giggles of the serving girls as they flirted with the young man ahead of him. He regarded the tall youth curiously as the latter smiled but remained polite. The young man appeared to be in his early twenties, a little over six foot tall, bronze skin, clean cut raven black hair, no facial hair, and wiry. He wore work boots, jeans, and a dress jacket. Interesting choice, given the peculiar nature of southern summers.

"So you're only in town for a few days?" the cashier smiled at him.

He nodded as the server put his order together.

"Business or pleasure?" the girl asked coquettishly while she worked on his food.

He took a deep breath. "Just visiting memory lane," answered a deep youthful voice laced with sadness.

That caught The Locator's attention. Like any proper southerner, the youth was respectful but unlike most of his generation he did not invite the attention of the girls. His manner was not receptive to their tacit offers. Naturally, his gentlemanly aloof manner intrigued them. Their eyes scanned for any sign of a partner: any jewelry or tattoo which would give clue to his status.

"What kind of memories?" the cashier ventured.

"My... my sister loved Huntington," he explained thickly. "I don't visit often, but I was in the area so I wanted to check out her old haunts."

The duo exchanged a look.

"Your sister...?" the cashier prompted.

"Three years gone."

A pregnant pause followed the information. Silently, the cashier proceeded to ring up his order. The server finished his meal prep and handed it over. Her eyes narrowed onto his throat and peered closer.

"Neat symbol," she remarked. "Does it mean anything?"

His shoulders sagged as he touched something. "It's for protection."

She glanced at him through her lashes. "Does it work?"

The young man took a deep breath. "More than you know," he confirmed before he thanked them for his order, nodded a polite farewell, and turned to leave. His hazel-green eyes met The Locator's. Just as Laurent did earlier, he felt the other take in his appearance and manner. The oddly familiar action set off a sense of recognition. The moment passed and the younger man left. He stepped forward and ignored the serving girls' disappointment at the young man's exit. Order complete, he sighed deeply once outside.

"Etienne Laurent?"

He raised an eyebrow. "And you are?"

The youth grinned, his jovial manner a stark difference from the somber individual in the shop earlier. "Benavidez." He gestured to the food. "We shouldn't eat here."

"Pardon?"

His gaze scanned the area. "I have a good place to eat, if you'll be kind enough to come with me."

'Well, that didn't sound ominous.' The Locator thought bitterly.

Aware of the older man's hesitation, the young man's next words helped build a bridge over the distrust. "How's the old warhorse?"

He blinked.

Benavidez chuckled and tapped at his necklace three times. "Leig."

Laurent's eyes narrowed at the younger man and then to the silver insignia To his surprise, it featured a familiar etching in the shape of a strange upright 'S' with a circle in the middle. "You're the friend he's waiting for?"

Instead of answering, his eyes darted to the Yolo Rollo. "Mind coming with me?"

Laurent froze for a moment. He was so young! A high school graduate most likely. If so, he should be en route to college, not involved in this dark world. Laurent blinked and shook off his paralysis. He had no room to talk. After all, he dabbled around this age. What started as a curiosity grew to a deadly hobby. Deadly because of what it cost him. His mind rebelled at the memory, and it took effort to refocus on the task at hand.

The young Hunter said nothing while The Locator gathered his wits along with his items.

They made their way to a separate eating area, sat across from one another, and set out their meals while they eyed one another warily. As they did so, Laurent examined the symbol. The illusion of the upright 'S' consisted of two arrows on either side of a center straight line. The first one direction arrow pointed to the left while the second single direction arrow pointed to the right and in between was a single line. The three were embraced by the circle.

Benavidez took a bite before he broke the silence. "Made any progress?"

Laurent redirected his attention to the task at hand. "I managed to visit Dead Ringer's old victims. He's made sure they had access to his new contact information."

"That didn't take long."

Laurent nodded. "Based on what Leig said, I imagine it's to make sure his little friend has access to a willing meal."

"I'd agree. At least his actions work in our favor."

"Only, we have a snag. They're not talking to me.

He must have told them not to share."

The young man regarded him curiously. Laurent chewed his meal as he considered the next move. Benavidez pulled something from his jacket pocket and slid it over. The receipt outlined a phone number, date, and time.

His eyes shot up to the face of his contact.

The young man smirked and shrugged. "I'm sure you know that personal tragedies come in handy in times like these."

The Locator did not have to ask what he meant. "One of the girls in Yolo Rollo got you the number?"

"Not proud of how I got this," he confirmed. "I don't like using people, but the Drude and Dead Ringer are feeding off pain. They must be stopped. Especially with Samhain happening soon."

Laurent scowled. Halloween meant different things to different people, but there were those who knew what Samhain was. Not to mention what could be done at this time. The number of fools playing with energies and forces they had no business reaching out to inevitably increased during this time. The amount of incidents and cursed objects birthed, like the World War II toy phone, during this window never ceased to amaze him.

Benavidez reclaimed the note. "The date is tomorrow night."

Laurent nodded grimly. "Best to contact Leig."

The young man chuckled dryly. "No worries about the old warhorse. He'll be there."

The Locator eyed the young man. "Did you know they would do that?"

"I suspected. After all, one of them is a close friend of a recent victim. The trick was to give a believable reason." The humorless smile which crossed the young man's features somehow saddened Laurent. "A number of skills are needed to Hunt. Believe it or not, acting is one of them. It helps blend in and, more importantly, gather intel or get close to a target."

"So, you're really a Hunter?"

He grinned and nodded again.

"But..." Laurent trailed off, abruptly unwilling to point out his age.

Benavidez accurately guessed the reason for The Locator's uneasiness. "Like I said, personal trauma," he supplied cryptically.

Laurent frowned but knew better than to pursue the matter further. He only knew tidbits about Hunters. They dealt with creatures most denied the existence of: cryptids, demons, paranormal beings, supernatural creatures, possessions, all that fun stuff. Like Locators, Hunters lived in the Hidden World and were very private. His friend Caz provided a few further details: they were Called, deadly, and possibly supported by an organization which provided funds and other resources. Caz learned this when his involvement in the occult resulted in a bad spade of trouble which required the intervention of three Hunters. In fact, not long after that, Caz dropped his occult dealings permanently. He occasionally shared his knowledge and contacts with Laurent, and determined this assignment would be more than The Locator could handle.

The Collector hired Laurent to retrieve the cursed toy. Laurent was accustomed to handling bumbling thieves, grief-stricken families, and even malicious cowards who used cursed items to kill. Unfortunately, a demon and a greedy human were tethered to this thing. An active partnership was new. With no idea what to do, and after his first encounter with the Drude, Laurent happily left the rest in the hands of the two Hunters. Problem was, he needed the item. He still had a job to do.

Laurent cursed under his breath.

Benavidez's brows rose to his hairline. "Something?"

"The Drude and Dead Ringer are using an item, a toy phone to be precise, as a lure."

The young man grimaced with disgust.

"They claim to allow people to talk to departed loved ones."

Benavidez scoffed.

He leaned forward to meet the other's eyes. "I need

that toy."

The young man gaped at him. "Say what?"

"I'm a Locator," he explained. "I've been sent to collect it."

The other scratched his temple. "Are you crazy?"

Laurent's short bark of laughter answered him. "I'm beginning to accept that I am."

Benavidez sat back and shook his head slightly. "Well, okay. So long as you agree."

"Just how will you deal with that thing?"

The youth frowned thoughtfully. "Leig and I will work together to separate the Drude from Dead Ringer first." He pursed his lips. "That won't be pleasant."

"Will the thing still be attached to the toy?"

"No."

Laurent inhaled deeply, relieved.

***

Four days after his first encounter with the Drude, Etienne Laurent once again found himself near Maple Hill Cemetery, neighbor to the Dead Children's Playground. However, this time he stuck close to Hunter Leig. Hunter Benavidez joined the group that traveled along the low wall which bordered the Cemetery until they stopped in the Playground.

"Are you sure about this, Lana?" a feminine voice asked tremulously.

"Trust me."

"Where is this guy?" Benavidez ventured. The young Hunter stood amidst them while his feet shuffled nervously. His acting skills showcased in the youth's uneasy manner as he scanned his surroundings with jerky motions and uneven breaths.

"He'll be here."

Dread enveloped Laurent. The trio did not anticipate a group of five: Lana, two girls, a boy, and Benavidez. The lure for him was to contact his sister. When they arrived, Lana refused to lead them in until the newcomer proved he brought enough large bills to pay the fee. Unfortunately, there was no sign of the target - Dead Ringer.

Laurent's eyes scanned the moonlit area eagerly, hunting for the man who held the cursed item. His hands clutched the special case the Collector provided. He yearned to see it again, even as he fought the need to touch the metallic surface. Leig warned him the sensation would return once the item was close. Laurent did not realize it would be so potent. How close was the thing? Laurent opened his mouth to ask Leig a question when the veteran quickly put a finger to his lips and pointed to the crumbling low wall.

The pungent aroma of rotten eggs accompanied by the sickening sweet smell of cologne wafted into the area. It preceded the rustling in the shadows beside one of the larger playground items which announced the Dead Ringer's presence.

"Ladies and gentleman." The dream peddler certainly had a flair for the dramatic as he emerged from the gloom opposite the group. Three jumped while Lana eagerly stepped forward. "Welcome." His eyes settled on the woman in front.

"I... we're here for Dead Ringer." Lana's voice trembled.

"So many?" He propped the suitcase in his hands. "Who wishes to go first?"

"I will!" the mother proclaimed.

"By all means." The dark man gestured her forward.

"Wait," Benavidez interrupted with an edge in his voice, "isn't there a price?"

The dark man smiled grimly. "The Veil has started to thin, making contact more possible." He shrugged. "You want to pass up a chance?"

"No!" Lana pleaded, at once reaching into her pants and pulling out money. "This is all I can spare. Please! My daughter..."

He cocked his head to the side and appeared to consider the offer but made no move to accept the measly fee.

Lana turned to the others, her eyes pleading. "Please..."

"Lana..." hesitation and doubt lined the girl's voice.

"It's real! You'll see. Just... help me."

They exchanged uncomfortable glances until the three pulled out their wallets to contribute. Lana quickly collected the loose bills with muttered thanks. The young Hunter did not move.

"A touching display of camaraderie. Who am I to turn away such an offer?" Dead Ringer declared with faux magnanimity. He placed the case on the slide, opened it, and put the World War II metal dual-receiver toy phone on one of its steps before he extended a hand for payment.

The mother quickly thrust the money into his hand and called desperately. "Leah Anne. Leah Anne. Leah Anne."

A blue glow pulsed in time with her words, each pulse stronger than the last. Finally, a faint haunting ring echoed. Three of the group huddled closer while Benavidez eyed the toy warily.

Lana sobbed and dashed for the phone. She picked the receiver up and began to talk. "Baby?"

An echo of a child's voice could be heard while an acrid stench increased. Lana continued to cry as she talked with the creature pretending to be her dead daughter. It turned The Locator's stomach.

It was when Lana staggered and fell to her knees that Benavidez rushed forward. He swatted her hand, which made her drop the phone. The bereaved mother glared at him through watery eyes. Her friends moved forward to surround her protectively.

"What're you doing?" Lana cried.

Benavidez's gaze never left Dead Ringer. "Get her out of here!"

"What do you mean?" the boy barked.

"Oh my God," a girl yelped, "Lana you're bleeding!"

Blood flowed not just from her nose, but also from her ears. Bloodshot eyes looked at the trio around her helplessly. "I need to talk to her!"

"Get her out!" the young Hunter urged as he stepped forward.

Dead Ringer froze for a few precious moments. When he moved to retrieve the toy phone, Benavidez launched himself. "MOVE!"

The two men collided.

Scared and confused, his words finally broke their paralysis. Lana fought feebly as she was dragged away from Dead Children's Playground. Laurent heard the mention of hospital while the aggrieved mother continued to struggle to return to the phone.

Benavidez and Dead Ringer wrestled to overpower the other. The young man pushed the dark man away from the cursed item while the other attempted to reclaim it. Once the quartet of victims exited the area, Leig emerged from their hidden spot.

Unlike his partner, he held his hands out and spoke a word. Instantaneously, a golden light encircled the toy. The Drude hissed and became visible. It cursed at the veteran who began to sing something in a low voice. In response, the air thickened and cooled.

Laurent finally approached. His job demanded he retrieve the toy phone this man used to lure people whose life force fed the Drude attached to it. The thing turned its attention to him.

"It'sss right there..." a voice hissed. "Your chansss to talk to her."

Laurent swallowed dryly.

"Take it!" it insisted. "Call her name three timesss..."

Automatically, his hand reached out for the small toy glowing on the slide's steps. The lure to talk to Natalie, his lost love. The desire to claim the opportunity to apologize to her. So close. Her voice was so close. He just had to pick it up and say Nat's name.

"Laurent!" Benavidez's shout sounded as though it were coming from a long tunnel. "Wake up!"

Simultaneously, the word 'Drude' joined Leig's song.

The glow from the protection circle washed warmth into Etienne. His hand hovered over the phone receiver before he physically shook himself. Laurent nearly fell for the trap. His eyes hardened and his jaw clenched.

"No." He decided aloud. His head cleared.

"Locator!" Benavidez ordered as he delivered a terrible punch to Dead Ringer's kidneys. "Help me!"

His sharp words broke Laurent from his deep thoughts.

"Don't let him break the circle!"

The Locator glimpsed the edge of a charcoal circle, where the golden light emitted from. Dead Ringer kept trying to get to it.

"Help me!" Heavy frustration lined his voice.

The Locator eyed Leig, who did not move and was focused on the toy. Whatever was going on, time was of the essence. Laurent dove for Dead Ringer to help Benavidez.

Leig's indecipherable song became more intense, the air so heavy Laurent could feel it.

A demonic hiss slithered around them as shadows tried to grab onto the veteran. Unable to grip him, it began to growl curses at him. Its partner managed to slip away from his two opponents and made a mad dash for the glowing toy.

"Keep him away from the circle!" The young Hunter hollered as he tackled Dead Ringer on his attempt to grab his treasure from the slide steps. Once they were on the ground, he rolled them away from the target. He ended up on his back, his arms wrapped under the other's shoulders and hands clasped behind his head. "Get his legs!"

Instinctively, Laurent dove for and grabbed Dead Ringer's legs. The other thrashed and cursed, demanding to be free. Unfortunately, the Locator was near his knees and was clocked a few times.

Leig continued to sing as the golden light intensified. Laurent realized the grizzled Hunter kept his body between the toy and the fighting pair. This close, he definitely heard the other singing with a baritone voice except he could not understand the words.

Dead Ringer howled in pain while Benavidez and Laurent held him. He struggled and cursed at them while the younger Hunter's voice joined Leig's in his strange song. The shadows came alive and wrapped around the duo. The darkness pressed, grabbed, cut, and struck the pair while they held down their human prey. Laurent watched as their silver insignias also began to glow with a golden light. In the distance, he swore he heard something like thunder, but he was not certain. The light wrapped the men in armor and deflected some but not all of the attacks. Throughout the assault, the mens' voices never faltered while the Drude continued to hurl curses at them. Gooseflesh tingled along Laurent's flesh as he felt a crescendo of power.

"Thisss isssn't the end!" It spit. "You'll never defeat usss!"

The two fighters shared a look of alarm over their struggling prey.

"Us?" Laurent breathed.

Benavidez shook his head, never breaking his song once he began.

The Drude cackled. "More will come!"

After what seemed like forever, both Hunters projected their voices in unison.

There was an ethereal snap and the dark man let out a final shriek before he fell limp. The darkness returned to normal. The heaviness around them lifted and the putrid scent cleared.

"Let him go," Leig instructed.

The two released the prone form. The three men stood and looked down at the now unconscious man.

"Now what?" Laurent asked breathlessly, his mind still trying to process what happened.

"We take him back to the hotel," Leig answered gruffly. "Got some questions for him."

"What about the Drude?"

Both Hunters looked grim.

"Don't worry about it," the older Hunter bit out. "Just take your booty to your crazy employer."

The Locator opened his mouth to protest.

"Leave it be," the younger Hunter added in a friendlier tone. "Your part in this is done. Let us handle the rest."

Leig gave him a sidelong look. "Unless you want to

graduate to Hunter?"

Laurent clamped his mouth shut and shook his head firmly. He approached the toy with trepidation. No glow. No acrid stench. It looked... innocent. He grabbed it and placed it in the Collector's special case.

Leig guffawed and clapped him on the shoulder.

"Let's get out of here," Benavidez muttered as he bent over to grab one of Dead Ringer's arms. His eyes met those of his senior when Leig grabbed the other arm. "We're gonna need help with the Druden."

The older man nodded grimly.

The sense of dread from before thickened.

For the first time, Laurent was glad he was only a Locator and not a Hunter.

END PART 2 OF 3
Join us in December for the Finale of "Drude"

Spectral Presence
DJ Tyrer

I sense it
Yet do not see it
This time
Every night
A spectral presence
Watching me
Two souls touching
One living
One dead
Connecting across the years
A mystery
That I fear to solve

ARTICLE

Brain Science Paranormal
R.D. Hayes

In a decade-old episode of the science podcast *RadioLab*, Stanford psychologist Lera Boroditsky describes a property of some human languages.

> There are languages that don't rely heavily on words like left and right, and some languages actually don't have those words at all. In the culture I got to spend some time in, they rely on North, South, East, West.

According to Boroditsky, approximately one-third of human languages, spoken by relatively small numbers of people scattered across isolated parts of the planet, have built into their grammars a property called **dead reckoning**. While studying a community called Pormpuraaw on Cape York, in Australia, she had what to an English speaker might seem like an anomalous experience.

> After about a week of being there, people were constantly pointing to locations and I was constantly trying to stay oriented. After about a week I was walking along. I was trudging through the sand. It was hot and I was thinking about whether I was wasting my time there or not. I wasn't sure if the study was going to work out. All of a sudden I noticed that in my head there was this extra little, it seemed almost like an extra window, like in a video game. There was a little console, and in that console was a bird's eye view of the landscape that I was walking on and I was a little red dot that was traversing that landscape.

Boroditsky stressed that this momentary map view, something that in other cases might be considered a psychic ability, was a case of her unconscious mind cognitively recombining linguistic information into a new experience, not unlike the way Geographic Information Systems software (GIS) can map more or less any form of data by simply layering them over spatial coordinates.

> They're using the same cognitive system that we're using. They're just using it differently. They're paying attention to something that we normally don't pay attention to.

In his book **The Head Trip**: *Adventures on the Wheel of Consciousness*, journalist and meditator Jeff Warren catalogued a dozen states through which the average person cycles in an average day. Waking, sleeping, and dreaming dominate our experience, but within waking (for instance) there are less common and less commonly noticed sub-states such as daydreaming, trance, and flow – the state of effortless fluid action that athletes call "the zone." There are also in-between states such as the hypnogogic, the transition from waking to sleeping, and the hypnopompic, the transition from sleeping to waking. These two transitions are not identical mirror images of one another. Sleep paralysis, the intrusion of frightening dream images into waking consciousness, is very rare in the former and more common in the latter.

Towards the end of the book Warren expanded this idea into a metaphor he called the Consciousness Mixing Board, imagining the brain as a musical recording studio with multiple channels on sliders. Every state we experience is a complex combination of activity in the underlying brain circuits represented by the sliders.

> Via expectations, suggestion and possibly even intention, we can remix our experience of consciousness. This is what the cumulative story of hypnosis, neurofeedback, meditation, lucid dreaming,

> psychosomatic medicine and others all point to. We can – in theory – learn to control levels of alertness, sensory resolution, lucidity in dreams – it goes on and on. What's more, we can actually remix domains of consciousness previously thought to be discrete – fire up dream imagery in waking, introduce waking lucidity into dreams and more.

Roughly twenty years earlier, in 1988, British author Colin Wilson made essentially the same basic argument in *Beyond the Occult*, the third massive volume in a series that began with *The Occult* in 1971 and continued with *The Mysteries* in 1978. He linked the various flavors of what most people assumed was extra-sensory perception with mystical religious experiences:

> Perhaps the most important aspects of these 'moments of vision' is that they suggest that there is a way of acquiring information that is quite unlike the ordinary method of 'learning from experience'. When the visionary faculty is switched on the mind seems to be able to penetrate reality — rather in the manner of X-rays — and to grasp meanings that normally elude it.

In some cases we can guess at the mechanisms of these "visionary" perceptions.

> Lombroso also came across the case of a girl who developed X-ray vision and asserted that she could see worms in her intestines — she counted thirty-three. Under treatment she excreted exactly thirty-three worms.

Since such worms attach themselves to the wall of the intestine with suckers or hooks, damaging the tissue, the intestine (which has its own neural network) potentially has precise information about where this damage is located. If that information happens to be propagated to the brain along the vagus nerve, the visual cortex could easily create an imagined representation of that intestinal worm-map, in a similar way as Lera Boroditsky's brain recombined linguistic and spatial information into a heads-up display of her location in a desert landscape. Perhaps this should not be surprising. The dreaming brain creates far more expansive, detailed, immersive worlds for us to move through multiple times a night. This speculative hypothesis would obviously have to be tested in detail, but that is what science does.

Other anomalous experiences such as precognition, telepathy, and remote viewing seem to defy the laws of physics as we know them. Earlier during the 20th century, scientific analogies for these experiences usually involved electromagnetism, in part because invisible waves seemed intuitively appealing as a possible mechanism, and in part because there were scattered anecdotal cases of people picking up radio broadcasts through metallic fillings in their teeth. The best documented case of this phenomenon was of a machinist whose teeth were accidentally coated in silicon carbide (a semiconductor) from inhaling dust from a grinder at work. Physicist Harold Puthoff tested the man and "cured" him by cleaning his teeth.

Today, as the electromagnetic spectrum has become more familiar and therefore mundane, explanations for psychic phenomena have generally shifted to the quantum realm, which still seems mysterious to the average person. According to Peter Bebergal, in his book **Strange Frequencies**, cutting edge technology always has a whiff of the supernatural about it.

> The 1933 Plew Television Ltd. Advertisement introduced their TV sets by announcing, "IT IS HERE," a remarkable transmission from the past heard in the Hooper film [*Poltergeist*]. The ad goes on to describe its Model No. 1: "The magic eye . . . the

enchanted mirror . . . The fantastic dream of ancient witches who were burnt for their dreaming."

The idea of breaking the rules of reality is so emotionally compelling that when science eliminates one mechanism for doing so, the imagination simply substitutes another. Indeed, in his multiple books and articles, anthropologist Pascal Boyer claims that ideas that violate the rules of everyday experience, such as immortality and many psychic or magical phenomena, are easier for the brain to remember, precisely because they break the rules. Exceptions are inherently interesting.

Otherwise, current neuroscience has little to say about these psychic phenomena. However, Colin Wilson also claimed that mystical experiences of universal connection and timeless beauty belonged to the nonverbal right hemisphere of the brain. There has been some support for this latter hypothesis, not least Harvard neuroscientist Jill Bolte Taylor's descriptions of her state of mind during a stroke to her left hemisphere in 1996, recounted in a popular TED Talk, "My Stroke of Insight," and later a book of the same name.

> We have the power to choose, moment by moment, who and how we want to be in the world. Right here, right now, I can step into the consciousness of my right hemisphere, where *we are*. I am the life-force power of the universe. I am the life-force power of the 50 trillion beautiful molecular geniuses that make up my form, at one with all that is. Or, I can chose to step into the consciousness of my left hemisphere, where I become a single individual, a solid. Separate from the flow, separate from you. *I am* Dr. Jill Bolte Taylor, intellectual, neuroanatomist. These are the "we" inside of me.

Wilson's 1988 book attempts to explain **all**

paranormal phenomena at once, an ambitious philosophical goal that is not congruent with the piecemeal way experimental science actually works. Even the paradigm shifts described by Thomas Kuhn affect only relatively small pieces of the overall scientific worldview at any one time.

Despite his ambition, Wilson is resolutely culture-bound by his Western philosophical training. For instance, in a massive 500-page book, he mentions Buddhism, which has thousands of years of experience with alternate states of consciousness, only seven times. Nevertheless, it contains much food for thought, and much inspiration for authors of paranormal or weird fiction.

> A person who is overwhelmed by the mystical experience could be compared to a person who is given a glimpse of a city from an aeroplane, and then told to make a drawing of it from memory. This is why the mystical experience is ineffable — not because it is impossible to express in language, but because our language is at present too crude.

Compare Wilson's quote to Lera Boroditsky's description of dead-reckoning languages above. To repeat:

> They're using the same cognitive system that we're using. They're just using it differently. They're paying attention to something that we normally don't pay attention to.

Obviously, Wilson's "visionary faculty" can not explain the full diversity of anomalous experiences, but it might account for a surprisingly large number of them. This is not to, say, *explain them away*, or to deny the importance of any one experience, but to understand that we as experiencers are larger and stranger than we prefer to acknowledge. Consensus reality as we experience it is not the purely objective background against which our experiences play out, but rather the smaller overlap in the Venn diagram between our larger subjective personal experiences. To paraphrase Jill Bolte Taylor and Walt Whitman,

>We are large; we contain multitudes.

REFERENCES / FURTHER READING

https://www.wnycstudios.org/podcasts/radiolab/segments/110193-birds-eye-view

Warren, Jeff (2007). **The Head Trip**: *Adventures on the Wheel of Consciousness*. Random House. New York, NY. https://www.headtrip.ca/

https://jeffwarren.org/everythingelse/illustrations/the-consciousness-mixing-board/

Wilson, Colin (2020). **Beyond the Occult**: *The Astonishing Conclusion to the Occult Trilogy*. Watkins, an imprint of Watkins Media Limited. London, UK.

Jacobsen, Annie (2017). **Phenomena**: *The Secret History of the U.S. Government's Investigation Into Extrasensory Perception and Psychokinesis*. Hachette Book Group. New York, NY. https://www.wkar.org/2017-04-19/secret-government-research-into-unexplained-phenomena

Bebergal, Peter (2018). **Strange Frequencies**: *the Extraordinary Story of the Technological Quest for the Supernatural*. TarcherPerigee, an imprint of Penguin Random House. New York, NY.

http://www.pascalboyer.net/

Bolte Taylor, Jill (2009). My Stroke of Insight: a Brain Scientist's Personal Journey. Viking Penguin. New York, NY. https://www.ted.com/talks/jill_bolte_taylor_my_stroke_of_insight

ARTICLE

The Zen Of Halloween:
A Holiday Of The Normal And The Paranormal
Gary Davis

Zen Buddhism is an Eastern philosophy that came out of the Indian subcontinent by way of China and then Japan. Known as *Ch'an* in China, it is primarily a fusion of Buddhism and Daoism that formed during the middle of the first millennium AD. Westerners know it by the Japanese name, *Zen.* Zen spread from Japan to the U. S. predominantly during the post-World War II era. It influenced counter-culture and peace movements in the U. S. and became part of the innovation philosophy of IT entrepreneurs such as the late Steve Jobs. Non-Japanese Zen masters became popular in the U. S., especially the late Vietnamese teacher and Nobel Peace prize nominee, Thich Nhat Hanh.

Zen is best known as a technique for the practice of quiet meditation, often called seated *zazen.* It is usually accompanied by deep breathing. The objective is to "clear the mind" and eventually achieve a sudden point of intuitive insight, illumination or enlightenment. Benefits may sometimes be realized after only ten to thirty minutes of meditation. One's ability to concentrate and focus can be significantly improved as a result.

Halloween, in contrast to Zen, is a Western cultural phenomenon, originating predominantly in Ireland, Scotland and Wales. It derives ultimately from the Celtic, end-of-October-beginning-of-November harvest festival known as *Samhain* ("sow-in"). Samhain celebrated the return of grazing animal flocks from upland pastures. Provision was made for food supplies over the coming dark winter months. Samhain may go back thousands of years to the prehistoric Iron Age and earlier, prior to Emperor Claudius' Roman invasion and partial conquest of Britain in the first century CE. Contemporary written documentation of ancient Samhain is lacking.

Halloween spread in the West primarily because the

popes of the Roman Catholic Church incorporated it into its calendar of holy or saint days during the first millennium CE in an effort to transform ancient pagan practices into acceptable Christian equivalents. Halloween, or Hallowe'en, is the eve (All Hallows Eve) of the November 1st All Saints Day.

Halloween has accumulated a wide variety of different traditions over the centuries, which can make for a confusing interpretation of its true meaning. There is the practice of wearing masks and costumes and decorating windows and yards with carved and lighted pumpkins (and lighting bonfires in earlier times). There is the tradition of playing tricks, or practical jokes, including damage to personal and public property. And then there is the practice, dominant today, of going from house to house asking for candy treats. This may be the oldest Halloween tradition, harking back to begging for "soul cakes" during the Middle Ages in return for saying prayers for the recently deceased, including on All Souls Day, November 2nd. Fortune telling became popular in the 1700s, as illustrated in Robert Burns' famous 1785 poem, "Halloween;" young women would play games to determine who their future husbands might be.

The relative importance of tricks vs. treats has varied over time. Halloween celebrations in the U. S. and Canada in the early 20th century featured lots of public rowdiness and mischief making, such as burning cars, knocking people over on sidewalks and bashing in streetlights. My late father once told me a story about hooligans lugging a man's car up to the top of his roof on Halloween night. (On a lighter note, my father bequeathed to me a Halloween postcard from about a century ago; it wishes the recipient "a Jolly Halloween.")

Adverse economic conditions during the Great Depression only made things worse. Cities had to shell out millions of dollars to repair Halloween prank damage. The year 1933 witnessed a climax to Halloween vandalism; the holiday that year became known as "Black Halloween."

Cities and towns in North America soon found a

clever solution to the excesses of Halloween tricks that didn't require abolishing the holiday. As a practical matter, the Halloween treat replaced the Halloween trick. The peaceful, door-to-door solicitation of candy treats, beginning around the 1930s, has been the American norm since the sugar rationing of World War II ended. However, even in the late 20th century, the fear of Halloween tricks never strayed far from the surface. Rumors of razor blades in apples and poisoned candy drove many young trick-or-treaters indoors during the 1970s and later. Parents began taking their kids to costumed treat events in church parking lots and large shopping malls. Halloween became "Malloween".

The history of Halloween is full of dualisms. Tricks vs. treats is only the most modern of these. There is also light vs. dark; Halloween falls between the summer season of long warm days and the winter season of long cold nights. There is the costuming phenomenon—people's normal identities vs. their costumed personages or "creatures" and "monsters" on Halloween. This is part of the Western tradition of temporary role reversal that occurred during other ancient festivals, such as the Roman Saturnalia of December 17-23, around the winter solstice; the high and mighty were often mocked during these celebrations.

More fundamentally, the duality of life and death is a perpetual undercurrent of Halloween celebrations. In ancient times, this was the distinction between the world of the living and the underworld/otherworld land of the dead. Celtic lore warned that the veil between the two regions was at its thinnest and most permeable on Halloween. Thus, spirits and supernatural creatures (the *Aos Si*) from the underworld could cross over into the world of life. In parallel fashion, people wore masks and costumes on Halloween to trick, scare or appease spirits from the other side. The popular "jack-o-lantern"—originally in Ireland a hollowed-out turnip or rutabaga carried by the wandering Jack—derives its meaning from the interplay of these two opposing realms.

Given all the dualities, one might legitimately

wonder where the true meaning of Halloween actually lies. Is the holiday an accumulation, over time, of loosely related traditions that simply amount to different ways of having fun on one day? Here is where Zen philosophy can make an incisive contribution. Zen is holistic; it strives for a clear understanding of all reality. As noted above, the achievement of such understanding is generally called "enlightenment" (*satori* or *kensho*). Nature is holistic also; it encompasses both life and death. Opposites in Zen are not only tolerated. They are integrated into one larger phenomenon or whole. An example is the well-known, full circle representation of the Chinese opposites, *yin* and *yang*, which goes back several thousand years.

The integration of opposites is related to another Zen principle—that almost all things are related to one another through multiple causation—the idea of *interbeing*. The relationship of nature to Halloween offers a good example of these Zen concepts. Seasonal changes of light to dark—of summer to winter—are not simply opposites but are part of one full, continuous natural cycle that is repeated every year. The air becomes chilly in autumn, and leaves change color and fall off trees. Grass turns brown and withers. The landscape appears more barren. Thus, death is an inherent, regular, ongoing part of nature. People don't normally think about this; death is treated as inconvenient and put out of mind most of the time in the modern West.

We do not directly celebrate death on Halloween. But symbolic representations of death abound and give the holiday its distinctive identity. Participants frequently dress as creatures or monsters—skeletons, devils, ghosts, mummies, zombies, etc.—that populate the mythological land of the dead. Front yards fill up with jack-o-lanterns, replica gravestones, white sheets, plastic skeletons and giant cobwebs.

The threat of a nasty Halloween trick adds an emotional dimension to this symbolism. Tricks have long been a part of Darwinian evolution in nature. Some insects, for example (e.g., the stick insect), have evolved to change color and shape to mimic their surroundings as a protection against hungry predators.

A household visited by multitudes of young trick-or-treaters may fear a trick if treats are not offered or it runs out of candy too early in the evening. Nothing deadly here, but someone's heart might skip a beat or two. Because of this implied threat, the costumed trick-or-treat creature gains a small amount of power on Halloween night—a sort of temporary role reversal. Adults may also enjoy an emotional release from acting out at their own Halloween costume parties.

The combination of all these practices and associated emotions makes for a Halloween phenomenon that is holistic in terms of Zen philosophy. Going further, the integrated nature of Halloween traditions is the reason why this strange holiday has survived for many centuries. At the deepest levels of myth, emotion and cultural meaning, Halloween has always been more than the sum of its parts. This is illustrated by the strong reaction of American families to isolated and exaggerated incidents of treat tampering several decades ago (noted above). Fearful of tricks in the local neighborhood, many parents switched their children to large-scale parking lot or indoor shopping mall treat-collecting events on October 31st. The sweet-toothed grin of Halloween has remained true to its ancient roots.

ARTICLE

**She Devil (1957)
Hair Color and Sensuality, Sensuality and Horror**
Denise Noe

This essay is dedicated to Mari Blanchard.

One of a multitude of 1950s blonde Marilyn Monroe imitators, Mari Blanchard never scaled to the Olympian heights of fame as the inimitable La Monroe, nor did she even reach the stardom of lesser Monroe-like blondes Jayne Mansfield, Mamie Van Doren (often called with Monroe "The 3 Ms") or Sheree North or Anita Ekberg.

However, Mari Blanchard stood out from the '50s blonde crowd with her distinctive, even quirky, beauty: wide face and large, wide-set eyes. Her more common but indisputably gorgeous features included high cheekbones and a sensuous mouth along with an hourglass figure.

Most importantly, Mari Blanchard catapulted to camp glory with the 1957 *She Devil*, a motion picture a sales website describes as a "sci-fi cult horror gem." This film gave its story a special spin by focusing on hair color. (The *She Devil* under discussion should not be confused with the 1989 Roseanne Barr comedy *She-Devil*.)

Like many films that attain cult status, *She Devil* had

humble beginnings, being theatrically released by 20th Century Fox on a double bill with another sci-fi flick, *Kronos*. A black and white flick made on a shoestring budget, *She Devil* is outstanding in neither direction nor pacing and possesses a script that can be refreshingly nasty but also pedestrian, turgid, and occasionally even unintentionally comic.

She Devil was based on a short story, *The Adaptive Ultimate* by Stanley G. Weinbaum, an author credited by sci-fi luminaries like Isaac Asimov with helping invent modern science fiction. Although Weinbaum died of cancer at 33, he left behind a respected body of work. Writer Jeffrey Kauffman observes that the "most notable" of Weinbaum's works is probably the short story "A Martian Odyssey." Kauffman elaborates, "Rather strangely, only one of Weinbaum's pieces has been adapted to various media, and even *more* strangely, it's been adapted a *lot*. Ironically this piece includes a form of 'adapt' in its very title. 'The Adaptive Ultimate' was published in November 1935, a mere month before Weinbaum's sad demise, but it went on to enjoy no fewer than three television versions, at least one radio enterprise, and the 1957 film *She Devil*."

Kurt Neumann directed, produced, and wrote the screenplay for *She Devil*. Film editor Kenneth George Godwin describes Neumann as a "journeyman director." Neumann is best known science fiction films like *Rocketship X-M* (1950), *The Fly* (1958), the aforementioned *Kronos* – and *She Devil*.

Fruit Fly Super Serum

She Devil starts with the screen filled with what appears to be a drawing of an insect. Then we see that we are gazing through the microscope of young, handsome Dr. Dan Scott (Jack Kelly). He jots notes as housekeeper Hannah (Blossom Rock in *She Devil*, credited as Marie Blake in some productions) walks into the laboratory with a meal on a tray. He brusquely says he is busy; she chides that he needs nourishment.

Looking outside the house, Hannah merrily exclaims,

"It's Dr. Bach!" An aging, thickset man, Dr. Bach (Albert Dekker) has returned early from a visit to Europe to the house he shares with Dr. Scott (there is no suggestion the men are anything but platonic friends).

Bach is soon in the laboratory with Dr. Scott. It is apparent Scott is Bach's scientific protégé. Scott confides that he wishes to prove that cure of disease or injury is "a process of adaptation." He considers the humble fruit fly the "most adaptive" of organisms so he developed a special serum from that insect. He has used it on sick and wounded animals – with wonderful results. He displays a series of formerly ailing/injured animals in cages that have been restored to health through the serum. However, there is one animal that suggests the serum may have an odd side effect. That animal is a black big cat. When Bach looks at a photo taken after the injury for which it was treated, he says he sees a tawny-colored creature. Scott explains that the animal's color changed shortly after it recovered and he is unsure whether the color change was related to the serum.

Anyway, he wants to experiment on a human. Will Bach let Scott experiment on one of the charity cases at the hospital Bach founded? The elder physician has reservations about the ethics of this but agrees -- providing the patient's prognosis is hopeless with conventional treatments and consents.

Bach soon finds the ideal patient: Kyra Zelas (Mari Blanchard), impoverished, unemployed, without living family or friends, and dying of tuberculosis. The black-haired woman is lying in a hospital bed, coughing and turning her head from side to side, when she agrees to the experiment.

The doctors leave her, as it will take hours before they know whether or not the serum has done anything. When they return – success! She has made a full recovery. The cured Kyra gazes admiringly at her reflection as Scott draws her blood. He is flummoxed that she does not even wince as the needle enters her flesh and, after he pulls the needle out, the tiny hole instantly closes.

Soon afterward, a nurse (Helen Jay) asks if the sun

hurts Kyra's eyes. "Nothing can hurt me now," she confidently replies.

Since the doctors are concerned about Kyra, they offer her a room in their residence, at least for a period so they can observe her. "Like a guinea pig?" she tartly inquires. They assure her that they do not consider her in that light. She agrees to the arrangement, adding, "Only because I want to. I'm only going to do what I want. I'm going to get everything I can out of life."

Bach gives her taxi fare. After she leaves, Scott marvels at her newfound assertiveness, saying she was previously a "quiet" and "timid" person.

However, she does not go directly to their home after checking out of the hospital. She goes to a boutique, wanting new clothes to go along with her new life.

In the store she, an older man (John Cavanaugh) watches a young lady (Joan Bradshaw) as she tries on clothes. He takes out a wad of cash to buy the clothes she wants.

Kyra approaches him, says, "I want that money," and grabs it. She clobbers him with a large, heavy ashtray. In the ensuing hullabaloo, she ducks into a dressing room.

In that tiny room, she switches her dress with one from the store. Then she stares at herself in the mirror. A miraculous change occurs, one she has seemingly willed: her black hair lightens until it is a shimmering platinum blonde! Explaining the behind-the-scenes technique, writer Glenn Erickson states, "The hair-color changing is a filter trick, an invention (camera operator Karl) Struss first used back in the silent era." No longer recognizable, she easily makes her way out of the store, stolen cash in hand.

When the doctors arrive at their shared residence, Kyra tells them she opened up an account using Bach as a reference and purchased a wardrobe. Hannah sardonically notes the quality of the clothing, adding, "And the lingerie – ooo la la!" Kyra explains her hair hue change as the result of a trip to a hair salon. "Your hair is beautiful – like nothing I've ever seen before," Bach admiringly says. It is obvious he has become enamored of his former patient.

Bach, suspicious of the hair salon story, surreptitiously picks some of the blonde strands from Kyra's hairbrush. Later, when he and Scott are in the laboratory, Bach puts them under a microscope. He sees no trace of chemical dye on the hair and surmises that the hair was not dyed but naturally changed color. Scott looks through the microscope and realizes Bach is correct. They both conclude that the serum that saved the dying woman's life has changed her in extraordinary ways. Much as the big cat went from tawny to black after taking the serum, Kyra has gone from brunette to blonde. Bach suggests that her glandular function has been unbalanced.

That it is Bach rather than Scott who initially sees through her lie about the hair being dyed in a beauty shop is a point that critic Kenneth George Godwin finds telling as it may indicate that a male "past his sexual prime" can more easily see through Kyra's lies. The young Dr. Scott is attracted to Kyra and, thus, more easily deceived by her.

Confronted with the next day's newspaper story about the assault and robbery in the boutique – and the tell-tale microscopic conclusions about her hair hue alteration – the defiant Kyra admits all and throws it in the doctors' faces: "You had no right experimenting with me. You created me and I'm your responsibility!"

They see truth in her assertion. Bach is dejected but Scott is worse than dejected since he has fallen in love with Kyra. That Kyra should enthrall Scott is understandable since, as Godwin aptly observes, Blanchard "exudes a cool sexuality which adds conviction to the character's power to overwhelm the male intellect."

A party is held to raise money for Bach's hospital. Among the assembled big shots are millionaire Barton Kendall (John Archer) and his elegant wife Evelyn (Fay Baker). Kyra saunters down winding stairs. Bach and Scott introduce her to the Kendalls. The wife compliments Kyra on her "lovely hair." Erickson comments that Struss "slightly over-lights Kyra in the party scene to make her hair seem to glow."

Not much later, Barton has escorted Kyra outside. As

Barton flirts, Kyra notices Evelyn approaching. Kyra suggests Barton may want to restrain himself. Barton retorts, "Evelyn is a very practical and a very understanding woman so naturally she's likely to overlook little things like this," and passionately kisses Kyra who pulls away from him.

Contrary to what Barton just said, Evelyn does not overlook this flagrant display. She furiously accuses Barton of causing a public scene. He replies, "I'm not causing a scene – you are."

"I'm not necking with this trollop!" the outraged Evelyn exclaims. (This is some of that "refreshingly nasty" dialogue referred to at the start of this essay.)

When Kyra expresses indignation at the epithet, Evelyn slaps Kyra. Without another word, Kyra hurries back up to the house, leaving Evelyn and Barton to spat.

Evelyn complains of being "humiliated" by Barton's misbehavior. Barton reminds her that he has often asked for a divorce and cannot understand why she wants to continue the marriage. "Does it occur to you that I might still be in love with you?" she asks.

He tells her he is sure she does not love him but the power and prestige of being a Kendall. She says that he can believe that if he wishes but, in any case, she wants the marriage to continue. Barton leaves the betrayed woman to lick her wounds alone.

A word should be said about the acting. Fay Baker's role in the film is brief but she does a superb job in depicting the betrayed wife, appropriately showing embarrassment, outrage, anger, and sadness. Indeed, one of the positives of this film is that it was well acted throughout by all participants.

The scene switches to Kyra before a mirror. She wills her hair to turn black; it does.

Then she hurries down to see Evelyn who cannot recognize Kyra. Kyra reminds Evelyn of the slap, and then strangles the shocked woman to death. Partygoers hear Evelyn scream. Looking out a window, Barton sees a black-haired woman rushing from the scene and asks, "Who the devil is that?" Perhaps "devil" was put in this sentence to refer to the title.

By the time other partygoers become aware of the murder, Kyra is again blonde. She hypocritically expresses sympathy for the victim – who has strands of dark hair clutched in a hand. She also reports seeing a "dark-haired woman" rushing away from poor Evelyn.

After the partygoers have left, Kyra quickly and brazenly admits her guilt to Bach and Scott, remarking, "She slapped me and I killed her and I'll kill anything that gets in my way. There's nothing you can do about it. You're just as involved in it as I am." She says she needs sleep and leaves the doctors to contemplate the horror they wrought when they tried to save the life of a pitiful T.B. patient.

In a later scene, Bach says, "She should have been allowed to die?" He says they did not "save the life of a human being" but created "an inhuman being who has no place in the human world."

Barton, who has no idea Kyra is responsible for his becoming a widower, courts Kyra. They enjoy a whirlwind courtship that soon leads to marriage. From her honeymoon in Europe, Kyra mails a painting that is a portrait of herself to Bach and Scott. Strokes in the back of the portrait vaguely suggest flames of Hades, eerily consistent with the movie's title.

Little time passes before Kyra tires of Barton and the marriage flounders. A scene is show of the unhappy couple in a cabin in a rural area. She complains of boredom; he complains of her coldness. She goads him until he shoots her in a fit of rage. Immediately remorseful and terrified for her life, he puts a towel on the wound and takes her to his car to driver her to the hospital. As he is driving, she shows him that her wound has completely healed. He has little time to express astonishment for she then causes a crash that kills him.

In their mansion, Bach and Scott hear a radio report about the car accident that killed "millionaire playboy" Barton Kendall – but from which his wife walked away unscathed. The physicians guess the truth.

Attired in the usual widow's black complete with veil,

Kyra allows the docs to persuade her to stay at their residence while they try to find a way to restore her to normalcy. She pretends to want to become a normal person again. However, when she catches Scott alone, she tells him she loves him and that the only thing standing in the way of utter success and happiness is Bach. Will the doctor she loves do his lady the favor of snuffing out that threat? He is evasive. When he later talks with Bach, he recounts the horror of Kyra's confident assumption that he would murder his best friend.

Unable to get Kyra to consent to an operation that might restore her to normalcy, the doctors discuss a way to put her "under" despite her adaptive powers. Bach points out, "No organism can live in its own waste products." This must be considered a singular failure of the script, as it seems to propose trying to suffocate Kyra in her own urine and feces! However, we are soon told that carbon dioxide is the waste product they will use to anesthetize her.

They administer the anesthesia and then a chemical they believe will return Kyra to normalcy. It ends up restoring her to her pre-serum state of dying of tuberculosis and this time she actually dies. They realize it is better this way as she was "meant" to have died.

Science Hurtles Forward, Flounders Backward

The most obvious theme of *She Devil* echoes *Frankenstein*. In Mary Shelley's classic, the ambitious Dr. Frankenstein aims to create life by electrically animating a body he has put together from human corpses. He succeeds in creating a life but instead of the beautiful, super-human being he envisioned, the scientist finds he has created an ugly, defective "wretch." As a scientist, he over-reached in playing God so his good intentions backfire. Kauffman observed that the "central conceit that Mary Shelley had exploited" was that "Man should not be poking his nose around in territory that should rightly be reserved for God" and that *She Devil* exploited that same conceit. Indeed, the basic idea of scientific hubris, the warning that human beings should realize their limitations and not attempt to usurp Deity or Nature, suffuses much science fiction and is certainly underlined in *She Devil*.

A secondary theme in the film echoes that of another classic, Robert Louis Stevenson's *Dr. Jekyll and Mr. Hyde*. As Dr. Jekyll liberates a primitive, monstrously selfish id from the restraint of superego/conscience and finds himself turning into the wicked Mr. Hyde, Dr. Scott endows Kyra with biological super-powers and, in the process, turns her from a presumably normal person into a violence-prone psychopath, a monster so coldly self-centered that she takes a life in revenge for a slap and is not the least bit bothered by following one murder with another.

Indeed, *She Devil* can be viewed as a kind of fusion of *Frankenstein* with *Dr. Jekyll and Mr. Hyde*.

Post-War Monster Women

In making its monster female, *She Devil* resembled many 1950s sci-fi and horror films. Woman-as-monster may have resulted from gender concerns common in the era.

During World War II, much of the able-bodied male population was required to risk life and limb to save the world from the Axis Powers. The need for manpower in combat meant a greater need for womanpower at the home front. Thus, many American ladies entered factories a la Rosie the Riveter and took a wide variety of jobs previously held mostly by men.

With the war's end, women tended to retreat to the home and male veterans to take jobs. For many women, becoming a housewife was wonderfully welcome; for many others, it was terribly frustrating. Moreover, women who wanted to enter occupations other than those traditionally female like teaching, nursing, and secretarial science often found themselves frustrated by day-to-day sex discrimination and the limited opportunities for them to advance in the workplace.

Those real-life female frustrations fed fears of female destructiveness. Thus, Hollywood released female fright fests: *Prehistoric Women* (1950), *Untamed Women* (1952), *Cat-Women of the Moon* (1953), *The She-Creature* (1956), *Voodoo Woman* (1957), *The Astounding She Monster* (1957), *Attack of the 50 Foot Woman* (1958), and *The Wasp Woman* (1959).

She Devil may highlight troubling aspects of traditional gender roles. Tom Weaver, author of several film-related books, observes that *She Devil* parallels *My Fair Lady* but instead of a man deliberately transforming a humble Cockney flower seller into the toast of aristocratic Edwardian London, a man inadvertently transforms a humble but decent woman into the most vicious possible vamp. Film reviewer Glenn Erickson points out that Scott and Bach talk to Kyra in a "paternalistic" manner sand more than once assure her, "We know what's best for you," a phrase that can been viewed as heavy with patriarchal condescension. Erickson also observes that gender roles are emphasized when Kyra steals money to splurge on a wardrobe because she is "simply taking care of business, getting what's necessary in a society that doesn't value a woman without material adornments."

She Devil at home among the "monster woman" films of the 1950s and the condescending attitudes of its men toward Kyra possess a "patriarchal" flavor, but neither these attributes nor the others already discussed adequately account for it its cult status.

Hair Color's Complicated Currents

The special aspect of *She Devil* is that it brilliantly links personality change to hair color, playing on the associations between a woman's hair color and who she is as a person. There has long been a fascination with women's hair – and not just in the West.

In 1978-1979, much of the world watched the Iranian Revolution on television and saw previously Westernized Iranian ladies show their allegiance to certain conservative interpretations of Koranic injunctions by hiding their hair, most dramatically under all-enveloping chadors and more "moderately" under scarves. In radical "women's liberationist" Kate Millett's account of her sojourn in the country, *Going To Iran*, she and women associated with her muse, "What is this thing about women's hair?"

It is not only Islamic conservatives who advocate female hair covering. The Bible has passages that have been interpreted as meaning that Christian women should cover their heads in public, or, in more common interpretations, during church services. Thus, in some churches it has been or still is expected for females to wear scarves or, more commonly, hats on their heads during services.

So just what *is* this thing about women's hair?

Hair can be beautiful. It has a sensual quality. It is good to look at and feels good to touch. What's more, the hair on the head may subtly remind people of the hair on the sexual parts of the body. Thus, covering the hair can be seen as modest.

The question remains as to why societies would especially focus on *women's* hair. After all, unlike, say, the chest area, hair is biologically the *same* on both genders. The answer to this might be that male sexuality is more "look" oriented while female sexuality is more "show" oriented. This is a matter of degree as girls and women like to look at those who attract them and boys and men enjoy being found attractive. However, since most people are essentially heterosexual, the higher degree of "looking" in the sexuality of the male and the higher degree of "showing" in the female may be responsible for a generally higher degree of interest in hair that graces the female

What's more, the hue of the hair, especially that of a female, has been invested with layers of cultural meaning. It even serves to identify the female. Although Susan Brownmiller's *Against Our Will: Men, Women, and Rape* includes some doozeys of nonsense, the wildest: "Rape is nothing more or less than the conscious process of intimidation by which *all men* keep *all women* in a state of fear," she makes a telling and true observation when she writes about media coverage of violent crimes, "Female victims are objectified and glamorized chiefly by the color of their hair while it is odds-on certain had little to do with their deaths." This writer, who grew up in the 1960s-70s, recalls female criminal defendants were also often identified by their hair color though it is odds-on certain it had little to do with the crimes of which they were accused.

While culture associates the brunette with being sultry and the redhead with being passionate and fiery tempered, the blonde is linked to a bewildering variety of personality characteristics. Indeed, an excellent book that deals at length with Mari Blanchard's life -- along with the lives of many fair-haired actresses -- *Fifties Blondes* by Richard Koper, is built around the special mystique of yellow tresses on females. Only blondes are apt to have "bombshell" and "goddess" affixed to them. Additionally, blondeness has come to be associated with stupidity, the phrase "dumb blonde" having entered the lexicon and "blond jokes" both playing on and perpetuating this stereotype. Why would intelligence be negatively associated with blondeness? There may be an assumption that blonde women, being most attractive to men, have less incentive than women of other hair hues to develop non-sexual skills since they are presumed to be able to survive and even attain affluence through their sexual power.

Gentlemen Prefer Blondes is the title of the popular Anita Loos novel that was turned into the popular Marilyn Monroe film. From *Fifties Blondes*: "But why do men prefer blondes? Maybe because blonde is associated with sex, fun and carelessness? . . . Blondes are girls that can give you a good time, without expecting much in return." Such associations led to "blondes have more fun" becoming a catchphrase in the 1950s.

The popular "blond bombshells" popularized the practice of dyeing hair blonde. However, at least at first, the practice was not completely respectable: "bottle blonde" carried negative connotations of phoniness, gold digging, and "easy virtue." Thus, there was a desire on the part of those whose blondness was chemically caused to present themselves as natural blondes, leading the Clairol company to advertise its blonde hair dyes with the teasing line, "Does she or doesn't she? Only her hairdresser knows for sure." In *She Devil*, when Bach asks Scott why Kyra did not disclose the truth about her hair hue change, Scott exclaims, "Don't ask me why women are so evasive about the color of their hair! They just are!"

It is possible Mari Blanchard was cast in the role of Kyra because Blanchard often changed her hair color during her career, playing a dark-haired beauty in several films and a blond in several others.

Curiously Be-Deviled Cast

Comment should be made on three of *She Devil's* cast members, two of whom lived lives that contained odd echoes of the cult film.

Less than a decade after playing her small role in *She Devil*, Blossom Rock/Marie Blake would become a fixture in America's living rooms for playing Grandmama in television's horror/comedy series *The Addams Family*. With her wild white hair and enjoyment of knife play, the madcap Grandmama Addams was a curious contrast indeed to the fount-of-conservative-wisdom grandmother of traditional folklore.

As noted, Mari Blanchard never threatened to topple Marilyn Monroe, but *She Devil's* cult status saves Blanchard from being forgotten. A look at her life makes it oddly poignant that she would be most remembered for a film about a dying patient saved by an experimental drug for Blanchard was haunted by medical problems throughout her life.

Born into affluence, Mari had an oil tycoon Dad and a psychotherapist Mom. As a child, little Mari dreamed of a career as a professional dancer. Those dreams seemed dashed when she was stricken with polio at the age of nine. She suffered from the illness for three years until recovering at 12. Then she spent years working to rehabilitate her limbs from paralysis. That work paid off and, when 17, she worked in a circus, riding elephants and performing as an acrobat on a trapeze. She left the big top to attend college, earning a degree but not using it for a career. She began modeling and was admired by famed cartoonist Al Capp who used her as the model for a *L'il Abner* character called Stupefyin' Jones.

Then Blanchard went into movies and TV. In 1954, she was cast opposite Audie Murphy in *Destry*, a remake of the 1939 Marlene Dietrich classic, *Destry Rides Again*. Because Blanchard was cast in the same role that Dietrich had previously played, the character's name was changed from "Frenchy" to "Brandy" and Blanchard played the role with dark hair. In a *Destry* fight scene, Blanchard suffered a real facial injury that necessitated medical attention. When filming *She Devil* three years later, Blanchard's scenes were interrupted by a real-life attack of acute appendicitis that almost killed her.

Blanchard continued in TV and film until playing her last role as town madam in the 1963 John Wayne comedy western *McClintock!* That same year, she was stricken with the cancer that she would battle until she died in 1970 at the age of only 47.

Albert Dekker, so believable as the caring and prescient Dr. Bach, ended his life in a manner suited to a scene in a violent movie. The tall, bulky Dekker was a talented, skilled actor who enjoyed a distinguished career on stage and screen. He is best known for playing in *Dr. Cyclops*, *The Killers*, *Kiss Me Deadly*, and *The Wild Bunch*. He had a side career in politics and served 1944-1946 in the California legislature.

A man who gave an impression of dignity, he suffered a remarkably sordid death. On May 5, 1968, he was found dead in his Hollywood apartment, naked and kneeling in his bathtub. A noose around his neck was strung over and looped around the shower curtain rod. Sexual terms were scrawled in red lipstick on his body. The coroner ruled it an accidental death due to erotic asphyxiation.

Although there was no evidence of forced entry, money and camera equipment was missing. This fed rumors of murder or a partner in kinky sex play who ducked out of the place. However, medical authorities believed the circumstances pointed to masturbatory play that went tragically awry.

Oddly, Dekker's death and others like it underline certain unpalatable but important truths about the human condition.

Few things are more powerful than sexual desire – except, perhaps, its distinct but closely related kin, romantic love. In *She Devil*, Scott is reluctant to acknowledge the truth about Kyra because he is in love with her. Barton Kendall repeatedly jeopardizes his marriage, reputation, and finances for lust. When his lust for Kyra ripens into love, he rushes into a disastrous marriage.

How does this relate to Dekker's death?

Solitary masturbation should be the safest possible sexual expression. There is no partner to reject or betray the masturbator, no chance of getting or spreading an STD, and no possibility of suffering or causing an unplanned pregnancy.

By practicing autoerotic asphyxiation, people turn what should be safe sex into risky sex and what can even be deadly sex. Dekker is hardly the only person who has done this. Actor David Carradine is another Hollywoodite who died in this manner. An article in *MedicineNet.com* estimates about 1,000 Americans die in this manner per year.

A desire for a sexual thrill led Albert Dekker to risk, and ultimately, lose, his life. He is hardly the only person to have turned masturbation – which should be the "safest" sort of sex – into something risky.

Sexual desire spreads the hurtful herpes and the life-threatening HIV along with a multiplicity of other sexually transmitted illnesses including those old stalwarts, syphilis and gonorrhea. Men sire children they cannot or do not support and, not infrequently, even though it means being incarcerated for non-support. Women with unplanned pregnancies go through the physical and often emotional trauma of (whether legal or illegal) abortion. They also suffer psychologically when they place babies for adoption or raise babies for whom they are unprepared to adequately care. Men and women both suffer for romantic love, which can lead to acts of violence including murder and suicide.

Despite the multitude of risks and costs associated with sexuality, it remains dearly valued by most people. Men and women alike continue to take those risks and costs rather then embrace celibacy.

Education is important but changing behavior is to a large extent a matter of willpower. Although it is worthwhile to warn people about the dangers associated with sexuality, we must realize that such warnings are limited in the good they can accomplish.

After all, writers and filmmakers have warned scientists for generations about the danger of scientific over-reaching yet it seems doubtful scientist will refrain from further exploration after viewing one of the multiplicity of versions of *Frankenstein* and *Dr. Jekyll and Mr. Hyde* – or the one and only camp classic that is the 1957 *She Devil*.

Bibliography

Albert Dekker (1905-1968). http://www.imdb.com/name/nm0215260/?ref_=tt_cl_t3

Brownmiller, Susan. *Against Our Will: Men, Women and Rape.* Ballantine Books. 1993.

David Carradine. (1936-2009). http://www.imdb.com/name/nm0001016/bio?ref_=nm_ov_bio_sm

Downs, Martin. "The Highest Price for Pleasure." MedicineNet.com. https://www.medicinenet.com/script/main/art.asp?articlekey=51776

Erickson, Glenn. "She Devil." *DVD Talk.* https://www.dvdtalk.com/dvdsavant/s4107she.html

Godwin, Kenneth George. "Five Shades of B." *CageyFilms.*

Oct. 28, 2015.
http://www.cageyfilms.com/2015/10/five-shades-of-b/

Kauffman, Jeffrey. "She Devil Blu-ray Review: Evidently Blondes Do Have More Fun." March 2, 2013. http://www.blu-ray.com/movies/She-Devil-Blu-ray/62195/#Review

Koper, Richard. *Fifties Blondes*. Bear Manor Media. Albany, GA. 2010.

Marie Blake. (1895-1978).
http://www.imdb.com/name/nm0086641/?ref_=tt_cl_t6

Mari Blanchard. *Glamour Girls of the Silver Screen*.
http://www.glamourgirlsofthesilverscreen.com/show/29/Mari+Blanchard/index.html

Mari Blanchard. (1923-1970).
http://www.imdb.com/name/nm0087080/?ref_=tt_cl_t1

Millett, Kate. *Going to Iran*. Coward, McCann, and Geoghegan. 1982.

Orloff, Brian. "David Carradine Died of Accidental Asphyxiation." *People*. July 02, 2009.
http://people.com/celebrity/david-carradine-died-of-accidental-asphyxiation/

She Devil. (1957)
http://www.imdb.com/title/tt0050958/?ref_=fn_al_tt_1

She Devil 1957 Mari Blanchard Scifi Cult Horror Gem.
http://www.ioffer.com/i/she-devil-1957-mari-blanchard-scifi-cult-horror-gem-139019081

Sindelar, Dave. "She Devil (1957)." *Fantastic Movie Musings and Ramblings*.
https://fantasticmoviemusings.com/2015/10/06/she-devil-1957/

Tooze, Gary. *DVD Beaver*.
http://www.dvdbeaver.com/film4/blu-ray_reviews_58/she_devil_blu-ray.htm

ARTICLE

On the History of Psychic Science...
Sonali Roy

It's absolutely impossible to exactly date when the psychic science emerged and developed. But Arthur Conan Doyle, in his *The History of Spiritualism*, vol 1, p.2, records that Emanuel Swedenborg "has some claim to be the father of our new knowledge of supernal matters." Swedenborg was a rationalist and lived in the world of the physical sciences. He had dreams and visions in his fifties and explored the spiritual world though a young Swedenborg had also experienced the visionary moments but with extreme reality and energy. Doyle says (p.2.),

> "Swedenborg was a contradiction in some ways to our psychic generalizations, for it has been the habit to say that great intellect stands in the way of personal psychic experience."

But, his psychic development, "in no way interfered with his mental activity", records Doyle (p.3.).

A natural mindset of Swedenborg was enough to drive him towards the other-worldly phenomena, "but what is not natural is that he should himself be the medium for such powers", states Doyle (p.3.). Though being a believer in Christian faith, Swedenborg thought "that virtue is not confined to Christianity" (Doyle, *The History of Spiritualism*, vol 1, p.5.). He considered all the evils as originating from selfishness. At the same time, he agreed with the 'healthy egoism' of Hegel. According to Doyle, Swedenborg's theological writings and his own practical experiences that he recorded attest that he had the clairvoyant powers, "where the soul appears to leave the body, to acquire information at a distance, and to return with news of what is occurring elsewhere" (p.6.).

In his first vision, as Doyle records (p.7.), Swedenborg refers to "a kind of vapour steaming from the pores of my body. It was a most visible watery vapour and fell downwards to the ground upon the carpet."

Swedenborg's friend, Cuno, a banker of Amsterdam, said of him, "When he gazed upon me with his smiling blue eyes it was as if truth itself was speaking from them" (Doyle, p.7.). Swedenborg's contemporary psychic observers confirmed the spiritual observations as made by Swedenborg. Doyle thinks

> "that he was subject to the errors as well as to the privileges which mediumship brings, that only by the study of mediumship can his powers be really understood, and that in endeavouring to separate him from Spiritualism his New Church has shown a complete misapprehension of his gifts, and of their true place in the general scheme of Nature."

Swedenborg's position in the spiritual movement is glorious and intelligible at the same time.

The 19th century US witnessed the surge of seances, telepathy, and clairvoyance that flooded till the 20th century although skepticism debunked such thoughts, beliefs, and feelings. There was a time when Americans carried on practicing and experimenting such things in their homes.

Some became curious to explain the scene behind the cognitive or other-worldly phenomena- they wanted to explore psychology and sciences of mind with the help of observations and technology and also included participants, who were aided with tools to measure their experiences. And though it was not flawless, rather futile according to scientific psychology, the effects are lingering.

Many periodicals in the 19th century like *Annales du magn´etisme animal* (1814-1816), *Archiv f ¨ur den thierischen magnetismus* (1817-1824), *Blatter aus Prevorst* (1831-1839), *Journal du magn´etisme* (1845- 1860), *Magikon* (1840-1853), *The Magnet* (1842-1844), and *The Zoist* (1843- 1856) etc. were purposefully founded to discuss trances, healings, and clairvoyance. A physician & mesmerist, John Elliotson, edited the *Zoist* and made use of it to safeguard mesmerism from the skeptics. The periodical criticized its critics and recorded many such examples of what could have appeared as induced feelings and clairvoyance phenomena in some intriguing manners.

In 1845 in France, the Baron Jean du Potet de Sennevoy, who edited the *Journal du magnetism* covering all aspects of animal magnetism, was especially interested in healing. One of many cases of medical uses of magnetism as included in the first volume of the journal reports that a patient was magnetised and a leg was amputated. There were also cases of healings supposed to have effectuated by magnetic action. One of the papers noted on the medical practice in the US treating bronchitis, dyspepsia, neuralgia, paralysis, and ulcers with hypnotic induction or mesmerism.

In the 19th century Italy, the two worth-mentioning journals *Cronaca del Magnetismo Animale* (1850-1860) and *Gazzetta Magnetico-Scientifico-Spiritista* (later called *La Salute*; 1865-1890) were run by physicians practicing hypnosis and allotted a considerable amount of space to discussing theoretical aspects of hypnosis. The journals also reported cases of surgical interventions with hypnotic analgesia, resolution of neurological and psychiatric troubles etc.

Another aspect covered by the journals is that they included articles on the appearance of spirits during dreaming and that thought was transferred after the hypnotic trance was produced and the senses also changed position.

In 1858, Allan Kardec founded *The Revue Spirite* for spreading spiritism in France. Kardec realized the need for "a special organ that could inform the public of the progress of this new science and prevent the exaggerations of credulity, as well as of skepticism" (Kardec, n.d./1858, p. 2). Kardec aimed at producing cases of visions & apparitions, intuitive feelings about the future, performance of walking, eating , or other motor acts while being asleep that the performers could clearly state, and the psychological phenomena at the juncture time of death. Kardec believing in the spirit interventions from the other world wanted to uplift his journal as a means for a systematized spiritistic movement and transcribe the moral and philosophical spirit communications because Kardec thought that knowledge of advance spirits could be beneficial for humans. He concentrated on the simple question-answers system to and from spirits of the deceased.

In other countries like England, many spiritualist publications came out, as Oppenheim notes,

> "By and large, the nonspiritualistic press reported the world of seances and spirits in a tone of condescension repeatedly questioning the judgment and critical faculties — not to mention the honesty — of spiritualists in general" (Oppenheim, 1985, p. 48).

Historically, the concept of mental mediums have been of immense significance for its considerable influence on the subconscious mind, dissociation, ideas of pathology, spiritualism, anthropology, and parapsychology. Individuals claiming to convey messages from incorporeals through automatic art, writing, visions, and impressions are known as mental mediums. Regarding the influence of the medium, John W. Edmonds, an American researcher, wrote,

> "I know of no mode of spiritual intercourse that is exempt from a mortal taint—no kind of mediumship where the communication may not be affected by the mind of the instrument" (Edmonds & Dexter, 1855(2):39).

In the mediumistic context, both the influence of the mediums and the discarnate influence are considered important, because these matter much in the entire process of mediumistic expression. The mediumship of Rosina Thompson was once discussed by Myers (1902), who proposed that mistakes and confusions may come "mainly from Mrs. Thompson's own subliminal self" (Myers, 1902:72). Myers also looked at

> "the influence of the sensitive's supraliminal self . . . whose habits of thought and turns of speech must needs appear whenever use is made of the brain centres which that supraliminal self habitually controls" (Myers,

1903(2):249).

There are also symbols in the context of mediumistic productions. As Hereward Carrington (1920) noted: "It is in the interpretation of these symbols that much of the true art of mediumship and psychic development will be found to lie . . ." (p. 109). He also commented that every medium "must learn . . . , by repeated experience, what the various symbols mean . . . , and thus form a 'code' or method of interpretation . . . . " (p. 109). As the analysis of the experiences of the mediums is concerned, Emmons and Emmons (2003) observes, "to a great extent mediums have separate 'psychic dictionaries'" (p. 258).

In his study of Mrs. Warren Elliott, Saltmarsh (1929) uncovers symbols. Saltmarsh puts,

> "It will be observed that the symbols are all of a certain type. They are what might be called natural symbols, and are based on habitual analogies, either verbal, as for example when the hallucinatory figure coming near to the sitter is taken to mean nearness of relationship, or common forms of speech, as when all black is used as a symbol for worry or sorrow; or else they may be natural pantomime, as when the gesture of waving away is interpreted as meaning that the ostensible communicator was not connected with the relic." (p.123)

How symbols are affected is also important- say of in respect to the general spiritual beliefs, or some specific interests that make a particular medium work in his/her sphere, e.g. how he/she is trained/and works. So, mediumistic communications depend much on individual differences/and the common patterns. It is also evident a medium learns about some specific topics/and images from his/her mental activities. Mediums used to work based on how they felt or experienced. The way they were affected by the changes was also an important factor. The effect could be both positive and negative. Maybe, their social surroundings impacted them much. Also, the instruments they used to sum up their experiences mattered much. A medium is said to have automatic brain-functioning that could "assume any personality, from that of a divinity to that of a toad..." (Rogers, 1853:171).

Later during the 19th and the early 20th century, the idea of hypnotism developed. As Delboeuf (1886) pinpoints, imitation and education could have influenced some hypnotic texture. There also came up the spiritualists, who started discussing about the mediumistic communications, although they sometimes expressed their doubts about the concept of reincarnation as the lessons of the spirits taught.

Further Readings:

https://med.virginia.edu/perceptual-studies/wp-content/uploads/sites/360/2015/11/Alvarado-Biondi-Kramer-Journals-EJP-2006-paper.pdf
https://www.researchgate.net/publication/281147632_Historiography_of_Psychical_Research
https://www.arthur-conan-doyle.com/images/4/4d/The-history-of-spiritualism-vol1-cassell-1926.pdf
https://med.virginia.edu/perceptual-studies/wp-content/uploads/sites/360/2015/11/Alvarado-Investigating-Mental-Mediums-JSE-2010.pdf
https://brill.com/view/journals/arie/22/1/article-p1_1.xml?language=en
https://www.ncbi.nlm.nih.gov/pmc/articles/PMC3552602/

www.ingramcontent.com/pod-product-compliance
Lightning Source LLC
LaVergne TN
LVHW012025060526
838201LV00061B/4467